TROMSØYA

Tromsøya

A Story about Sami Christmas Spirit

Leith Harte

Paperback ISBN: 978-1-9162199-6-0
E-book ISBN: 978-1-9162199-7-7
Hardback ISBN: 978-1-9162199-8-4

The people, places, and events in this story are fictional. Some historical events are quoted to provide context for the story. Facts and timescales have been altered for narrative effect. All inaccuracies are the author's responsibility.

This book is dedicated to Roar Nyheim and Karen Kemi, Sami guides I met at Camp Tamok. Roar prefers the world when the temperature is forty degrees below zero.

Nothing in life is to be feared. It is only to be understood.
                                    —Marie Curie

Contents

Chapter 1

Tromsø

Flying in blizzard conditions is unusual in England. In a country that once had an empire covering a quarter of the planet, a blizzard will ground every plane for days. This is not the case in Norway.

Jean and Kenneth Everton flew out from Manchester in the bright sunshine of an English winter morning. They were flying to the Norwegian capital city, Oslo, and then farther north from Oslo to Tromsø, on Norwegian Airlines scheduled flights. It was December 21.

There was not a speck of snow anywhere in northern England as they took off. They flew through clear skies for most of the first leg of their journey, but the skies grew darker as they flew north. They then flew on to Tromsø in a much smaller plane, with propellors instead of jet engines, crossing the arctic circle and entering the land of permanent winter darkness. Snow started falling during their second flight, as if the Arctic wanted to warn them about where they were going, or possibly welcome them. The last sunrise in Tromsø had been in late November, and the next would be in mid-January. For the second flight, they could see little, due to the permanent winter night and falling snow.

Flights to Tromsø, a city on the island of Tromsøya in northern Norway, are an interesting experience for travellers from the south. As they approached the end of their journey, the town's lights were invisible to them as their small plane approached Tromsø airport. When the runway was less than ten feet below them, they could just make out the snowy grey fields and the runway lights through the thick blizzard.

Temperatures in Tromsø in December average twenty-five degrees Fahrenheit, or minus four degrees Celsius. This is relatively warm for most of Norway but cold for those from a temperate climate, such as England. Since the temperature rarely rises above freezing in this part of the world, from October there is plenty of ice and snow covering Tromsø and the surrounding area. Roads and runways are icy and slippery for many months. Snowfall of one or two inches each day is common, which builds up to a deep layer in the countryside. Snow ploughs clear the roads every day in the city and in much of the countryside, but they remain icy and slippery for normal tyres. The drivers of Norway are more than a match for these conditions. All vehicles in Norway have steel studs in their tyres to enhance grip. Pavements in Tromsø are cleared daily by an army of apparently invisible labourers, for the workers and tourists. Norwegian natives, shoppers, and tourists walk around the town easily, visiting restaurants and shopping, wrapped warmly in their insulated coats, boots, and hats.

The landing was perfect, despite the ice and snow. The Evertons hardly felt the wheels touch down. For Norwegian pilots, this was just a routine day.

As Jean and Kenneth disembarked from the plane, they could barely see the terminal building ten paces away. The bitingly cold snow hit their faces as they hurried into the shelter of the building, painting lines in newly fallen snow with their hand luggage.

"I knew it was going to be dark, but it still seems a surprise that it's so dark and cold out there so early in the day," said Jean.

"Yes. It's daytime, yet it's also night. Spooky, really. Especially coming from a bright and sunny England. Hopefully, this means we will get an especially clear and brilliant view of the northern lights," said Everton.

They stood by the carousel waiting for their suitcases with the other passengers. Most of them were chatting in Norwegian. Despite this, the newscaster on the television mounted on the ceiling was announcing the news in English.

"There seems to be an outbreak of some form of illness in New York," said Jean, looking up at the screen. "It must be serious. Those doctors are dressed in bubble suits."

Everton was trying to lift a large suitcase from the carousel but was struggling. The suitcase had become wedged between the moving carousel and another piece of luggage. As he tried to lift it, he was pulled along with the flow of luggage. Other passengers had to move out of his way as he pulled in vain at his suitcase. He became a human plough, casting fellow passengers aside as his suitcase dragged him behind it.

A small and seemingly elderly lady was in his way, but instead of stepping back, she stepped towards him and grabbed the handle of Everton's case. Her hand overlapped with Everton's, and for a brief moment, their hands touched. Everton immediately felt a glow of friendship emanating from the old lady. It was more than friendship, though. He also felt a keen intellect and a deep curiosity reaching out to him. His eyes locked on to the bright blue eyes of the elderly lady. They smiled at each other as her hands closed on the suitcase handle. They were both pulling together, and with this additional help, the suitcase came free immediately. Everton and the lady lifted it off the carousel together. Everton let go of his suitcase and stood upright, looking down at the lady. She was at least a foot shorter than him and at least thirty years older.

"*Takk*. Thank you," said Everton.

The lady wore a fur coat, fastened up to the neck, and a brightly coloured woven hat. Jean and Everton had picked up a smattering of Norwegian from a TV detective series based in Scandinavia and from brief online Norwegian classes before their trip.

The elderly lady smiled up at Everton. Her face was deeply wrinkled, and her grey hair was cut short. "Vær så god. Velcome," she replied. She patted Everton on the arm in a sympathetic gesture, as if she recognised how difficult it was to be such a weak man, needing the help of an old lady to retrieve his suitcase. She turned away and walked to the exit gate, carrying only a small handbag over her shoulder.

"Now that is very odd," said Jean. "If I didn't know better, I would have thought that lady recognised you. She treated you as if she was your mother and you needed her help. Did you recognise her?"

"I've no idea what you're talking about," said Everton. "How would I know an old Norwegian lady on my first-ever trip to Norway? She was just…just very friendly, I think."

"Well, it was certainly lucky that a small, elderly lady was available to help you lift that suitcase," said Jean, smiling. "I don't know what you would have done if she hadn't been there to help you out. I might have had to lift it for you."

"I must have touched some kryptonite on the flight," said Everton. "My superpowers seemed to fail me temporarily."

The next suitcase was less problematic, or Everton had recovered his superpowers. Jean and Everton were soon through the exit gate waiting in a short but snowy queue for a taxi.

"Welcome to Tromsø," said their taxi driver in perfect English, opening his boot.

"Hotel Clarion Edge please," said Jean, as they buckled their seat belts.

"No problem," said the driver. He swung his taxi onto the main road, which crossed the island of Tromsøya from the airport to the town of Tromsø. The blizzard continued during their taxi journey. Despite this, the traffic was travelling smoothly at fifty kilometres per hour. Icy roads and falling snow seemed to be no hindrance to the drivers.

"In England, this weather would have stopped all traffic for weeks," said Everton.

"Ah yes. We read about your special leaves in England. A leaf can stop a train in London. Yet you were able to win two world wars. In Norway, we are puzzled by the way the English allow the weather to beat them. We are used to this weather, of course," said the driver. "We have special tyres, which are very grippy, with steel claws in every tyre. We also clear the road very often. Our snow ploughs are the best in the world. Only the Canadians are even close to ours. Many times every day we clear our roads. On the island of Tromsøya, we also have magic tunnels that we use in the very heavy snow and in heavy traffic."

"So this isn't heavy snow?" said Jean.

"No. This is just a minor snow shower," said the driver, chuckling.

The taxi entered the tunnels, which weaved under the hill at the centre of the island and under the city of Tromsø. The large tunnels were snow free and well lit. Traffic was flowing freely. The taxi continued for several miles, then emerged into the centre of the shopping district of Tromsø.

"You are here for the reindeer? Or perhaps the northern lights?" said the driver, his bright blue eyes looking in his mirror at Everton.

"Absolutely. We are hoping to see the lights," said Everton. "Hopefully, we will get a good display."

"I think so. We have been seeing northern lights in the middle of Tromsø for the past few nights. If you get out into the country-side, it should be very good. Very bright and clear. Did you know that the northern lights are mentioned in the Old Testament? Some of the Sami people believe that the lights are the souls of dead people and that they have magical powers. But you are not supposed to wave or whistle at the lights. This is considered dangerous by superstitious people."

"Very interesting," said Jean. "Thanks for warning us. I thought we knew that the lights were due to charged particles in the upper atmosphere, caused by solar wind."

"Yes, I think you are right about this," said the driver, with a broad grin. "Some of our scientists claim this. But some Sami also say that the lights are caused by a magic fox running across the sky. They say you can hear the lights if you listen carefully. Dead souls, magic fox, solar wind. Take your pick. Myself, I prefer the ancient legends. Much more interesting. I am from a Sami family."

Jean and Everton hurried from their taxi into the warm lobby of their hotel. Their room was on the seventh floor, with good views of the town.

"We finally made it," said Jean, once they were settled into their room. "A well-earned Christmas reward and a break from a crime-solving career for you." She stepped close and hugged Everton. Her head rested on his chest, a foot below his. "I am glad you decided to ask for a sabbatical break," said Jean. "You've worked hard enough and earned it."

"I wasn't too sure at first. But you convinced me. I have warmed to the idea. Getting away from the criminal world, and from boring police bureaucracy, is refreshing. This trip should be stress free and calming for both of us. And I hope we experience the delights of arctic winter. Wildlife, dogsledding, northern lights, and Sami traditional life," said Everton, returning the hug.

"Yes indeed. I hope this is the start of many similar trips to exotic destinations," said Jean.

Jean spread out her travel documents on the bed and started reading. "Most of Tromsø is built on the small island of Tromsøya, connected to the mainland to the south by two bridges and connected to a larger island to the north by another bridge," she said, reading from a booklet. "This provides fishing boats with a relatively sheltered position. The Gulf Stream reaches the arctic circle here and flows past Tromsøya, keeping the coldest weather at bay, which encouraged settlers. Tromsø is actually one of the warmer parts of Norway. The island has marked the border between the Norse people to the south and the Sami people to the north for over a thousand years."

"Well, if Tromsø is a warmer part, the rest of Norway is going to be really cold. We are going to need all this winter clothing we brought," said Everton.

Their hotel room looked south across the water to the mainland. Jean and Everton stared out the window at the sparking lights of the city. It was early afternoon and pitch black outside. The sun would not rise again here for many weeks. Beyond the lights of the city, the surrounding countryside was concealed by the darkness of the arctic winter.

The temperature outside was sinking as the snowfall was easing. Jean and Everton decided to venture out to see the city before dinner. They struggled into their thermal undergarments, neck and face warmers, double socks, double gloves, sturdy waterproof boots, and thickly insulated parka coats. It took half an hour just to prepare for departure. Once insulated, they ventured out into the streets of Tromsø.

Despite the temperature and the weather, the streets were filled with tourists and shoppers.

"As they say, there is no such thing as bad weather, just the wrong clothes," said Jean, linking arms with Everton.

"Let's take a look in here," said Everton, coming to a halt outside a brightly lit shop that was bursting with animal-skin arctic clothes and footwear.

"I know what you want. You're looking for a fur hat, aren't you," said Jean.

"Well, you never know when you will need something better than these artificial, man-made hats, or woollen caps," said Everton.

"Actually, I think you will find that fur hats are still man made. Foxes don't make them for us. Men borrow the skin from a fox first, without the fox's permission," said Jean.

Everton shrugged, and they both stepped into the shop. Everton took off his thick, woven cotton hat, scratched his head, and looked around for the hat section.

He became aware of someone staring at him. An elderly lady was standing at the end of one aisle, just watching him.

After a few seconds, she approached Everton and spoke in Norwegian. Everton had no idea what she had said, but he was fully prepared.

"*Hatt. Rev. Tetning. Reinsdyr.* Fox, reindeer, or sealskin hat?" said Everton, pointing at his head, then at his cotton hat, which he held in his hand.

"Ja, Ja, fox, reindeer, and seal. Warm for head," replied the woman, and she beckoned for him to follow. She led him to a rack on which various hats were hanging. "Fery goot. Fery varm. You will need this, where you go," said the woman, pointing to the hats.

Everton looked at Jean and smiled.

Ten minutes later he stood at the checkout with a fox-fur hat with large earflaps.

Everton put on his new hat, carrying his cotton English cap in the carrier bag. "Wow, this is warm as toast," he said to Jean, grinning widely. He looked into the window of the shop and moved from side to side, trying to catch his reflection, to inspect and admire his new hat.

"Did you notice? I think that was the same lady who helped you with your luggage at the airport. If I am right, that is a bit of a coincidence, don't you think?" said Jean.

"Really? I suppose she looked similar. But slightly different with indoor clothes," said Everton. "Perhaps she is my Tromsø stalker?"

The snow had stopped, and the sky overhead was black. Jean and Everton strolled down the street, past shops and cafés, each lit with a warm and inviting glow.

"*Storgata*," said Jean, looking up at a street sign. "I think this means Big Street or Great Street."

"Sounds more like 'the gateway to stores' to me," said Everton. "Something that should delight you. The gateway to infinite pleasure."

As they looked up, ribbons of pale light green and blue light started to ripple in the sky along the line of Storgata.

Jean and Everton both opened their mouths and stared in the ancient international custom of tourists as the ribbons of light weaved backwards and forwards across the sky.

"Wow. We are only in Tromsø for a couple of hours, in the middle of a well-lit street, and we already see the aurora borealis," said Everton.

"Pretty amazing," said Jean. "I bet this would be even better out in the countryside."

As quickly as they had appeared, the lights flickered and disappeared.

"Let's get a hot drink," said Jean, pulling Everton's arm towards the warm orange glow from a coffee shop.

They sat at the window of the café, watching the passing shoppers outside and nursing their warm mugs of hot chocolate. A television was mounted above the coffee bar. The newscaster was speaking in English.

"Listen to that," said Jean. "Something about that outbreak of illness in New York. Now they are reporting similar cases in London too. The doctors are saying it might be some form of haemorrhagic fever. Isn't that what Ebola is?"

"I think you're right. I thought Ebola was only in Africa. How would it get to London and New York?" said Everton.

They both listened for a few minutes to the newscaster. There were pictures of health care workers, dressed in bubble suits, wheeling a patient into a hospital. The patient on the trolley was not moving.

"Doesn't look good for him or her," said Everton. "I think the mortality rate for Ebola is very high."

"Yes, but I thought that it was quite easy to keep the infection confined to small areas or groups because it is so severe. It is one of those infections for which it is easy to spot the signs, and the patients are so ill they don't move around much before they die, rather fast. It is kind of self-limiting," said Jean. "I think that's right. I hope they contain it."

Jean and Everton looked at each other for a moment. Then turned their attention back to their warm hot-chocolate drinks.

"So, what's the schedule?" said Everton.

"Dinner tonight at the hotel, I think," said Jean. "And one of our guides wants to meet us at the hotel for an introduction this evening. Tomorrow morning we meet up with the guides and our fellow tourists for some safety instruction. Then, tomorrow afternoon we are off into the countryside and the mountains for a northern lights trip. The following day we will be dogsledding with a Sami family out to a Sami camp, where we will stay over Christmas. I think we cross to Finland, and possibly Sweden, during the sledding, but there are no border controls for the

Sami out in the wilderness. While we are staying with the Sami, we can try a snowmobile trip, reindeer herding, and, of course, traditional Sami food."

"Safety instruction. Sounds quite serious. More than just warm clothes in this climate, I think," said Everton.

"We certainly will need warm clothes. The safety stuff is just in case anything goes wrong, of course. You know that. But we will be with experts, Sami people, who live in arctic conditions all year round. The Sami have occupied northern parts of Norway, Sweden, and Finland for thousands of years. They are seasoned experts in arctic survival. They thrive up here during months of freezing darkness."

"Right. Err. I don't want to be a bore. But before we go back to the hotel, would you mind if we popped into the police head-quarters? Its only ten minutes' walk from here. I just want to make a courtesy call on some colleagues here in Tromsø," said Everton.

Jean stared at Everton hard for a few seconds.

"I don't believe it. This is supposed to be a sabbatical break and a holiday for both of us. Visiting the local police station is not my idea of fun in Norway. Anyway, how do you know anyone in Norway? You haven't been working with Norwegian police. Have you?" said Jean.

"No, no, not really. Just some people I have met at various meetings over the years. Literally just popping in to say hi. You don't have to come in with me. It will be over before you blink. I promise, it will only be a ten-minute walk and an even shorter chat. Scout's honour."

"Do I have a choice?" said Jean, standing and pulling on her hat.

The walk to and from the police headquarters along the waterfront was icy but scenic. They passed the two-kilometre bridge over the arctic inlet separating the island from the mainland.

Everton was true to his word. He was buzzed through the security barrier at the police station. Jean remained in the reception area. Everton spent only ten minutes in the police building before returning to Jean in the lobby, mumbling apologies for interrupting their holiday.

"Was that really worth it? You only spoke to your colleagues for a few minutes. I can think of ten thousand things we could have done rather than visit this boring police building. I don't know why you bothered," said Jean.

"I agree. Won't happen again. Thanks for being so patient. I will make it up to you," said Everton.

As they walked back towards their hotel, snow had started falling again. They linked arms and crunched through the new-fallen snow.

"That is the Ishavskatedralen. The Arctic Cathedral," said Jean, pointing out the brightly lit triangular landmark on the mainland across the bridge. "We should call in there when we get back from our arctic safari with the Sami people."

They retraced their steps along Storgata and passed a small square with a large Christmas tree, brightly lit in the centre. A choir of well-wrapped Norwegians was singing carols next to the tree. Jean and Everton paused and savoured the atmosphere.

"This is a fairy-tale location," said Everton.

"What more could you wish? A new fox-skin hat, northern lights, a Christmas tree, and live outdoor Christmas carols, all in one afternoon," said Jean. "Topped off with a boring visit to a police station."

Everton breathed in and nodded. "Yes. Grovelling apologies once more. I wouldn't dare suggest any more rubbish about work. Not even the slightest mention of police or criminals. All traces of work are erased from my mind forever. The whole setting is fabulous. I bet we see the northern lights every night as well. I mean every day and night, of course, since day is night and night is day up here."

"You may be right," said Jean. "Let's hope so."

Back at the hotel, they enjoyed a relaxing dinner. They both chose reindeer steaks.

"Interesting. Mild and sweet tasting. Not at all fatty. Reindeer meat is supposed to be very healthy. And the rate of heart disease in Sami reindeer herders is apparently very low," said Jean.

They were sipping two small shots of akvavit, a Norwegian brandy, when a man approached them, leading a lady and two children. "Good evening. My apologies for interrupting. My name is Vulle Issákson. I think you are Mr. and Mrs. Everton, yes?" said the man.

"Indeed," said Jean. "We were expecting to see you. This must be your family."

"Ja. Yes. We wanted to introduce ourselves. We will be travelling with you for a few days with our dogsleds. You will become part of our extended family," said Vulle. "I want to introduce you to my wife, Ánne. And this is Oskár, my son, and Sárá is my daughter. They are young, but they are very experienced travellers with our dogs. They will be helping you to drive your dogsleds and get to Camp Trollfjell."

Vulle was a stocky man, a few inches less than six feet tall. He had short, light brown hair, greying at the side, and steely blue eyes. In his hand, he held a fox-fur hat, similar to Everton's. He had wide shoulders and large hands, which looked like they had seen outdoor work. Ánne was shorter than Vulle, just over five feet tall, with similar piercing blue eyes and medium-length light red hair. Oskár appeared to be about twelve years old, slightly taller than his mother, with short blond hair and blue eyes. Sárá was several inches shorter than Oskár, perhaps ten years old, and shorter than her mother, with long, straight, almost white-blond hair and the family trademark piercing light blue eyes. All three of them waved and smiled at the guests as they were introduced.

"We all speak English, especially my children, but you can practise your Norwegian or your Sami with us too if you want," said Vulle.

"Please join us," said Everton.

The Issákson family all drew up chairs from surrounding tables, and they crowded around the table with Jean and Everton.

Little Sárá quickly jumped into the chair next to Jean.

"My name is Jean, and this is Kenneth," said Jean. "Most people call him Everton, but you can just call me Jean."

They ordered hot drinks for the Issáksons. Oskár wanted a shot of akvavit, as was natural for any boy of twelve, but this was vetoed by his mother.

"I hope you don't mind. Can I ask what you do for work?" said Sárá to Jean.

Jean was surprised by this question from the tiny girl. "Of course. I work as a talking therapist. We call it a clinical psychologist. You might know my job as a counsellor. I help people who have broken minds to get better," said Jean.

Sárá nodded as if she understood this perfectly, and it did not seem at all unexpected. "And what do you do for work, Mr. Everton?" she asked, looking directly at Everton.

"I am a detective. A sort of policeman. I try to stop naughty people from doing bad things, or I try to catch them if they are naughty," said Everton.

Again Sárá nodded, as if this, too, was no surprise to her.

"Do you know much about Norway or about travelling by dogsled?" said Vulle.

"Not much, really. We have read a little from the travel guide, but this is a really new adventure for us," said Jean.

"The Sami people have many traditions and customs that you will find interesting. We will teach you how to drive the dogsled. You might learn how to catch a reindeer and to check if it is healthy. We can tell you about our Sami legends and our religion if you are interested," said Vulle.

"That will be very interesting. We would like that. Isn't that right, Kenneth?" said Jean, turning to her husband.

"Yes. Absolutely. Very interesting," said Everton.

"Sárá is a bit of an expert on Sami folklore," said Ánne. "She will keep you awake all night if you let her tell you her tales."

"Would you like to know something about our legends and our gods?" said Sárá.

"Yes. That would be very nice, Sárá," said Jean. She moved her elbow to jog Everton's elbow.

"Err, yes. Absolutely. Of course. Tell us about your gods," said Everton to the tiny girl.

Sárá beamed at the two tourists and took a breath. "Well, we have stories about many gods," she said. "Most of these are gods who control the weather. The weather is a big thing for us. It is often the difference between life and death. We have the thunder and lightning god, which you might find interesting. But we also have gods for wisdom. Wisdom is a big thing too. People are always searching for wisdom. Wisdom, wisdom, wisdom. Of course, this is self-evident. Nobody ever said that wisdom is rubbish. To the Sami, making good decisions is very important. This is probably important to all people, actually, but I can't be sure, since I haven't met most people."

Sárá paused to make sure that her audience was still listening and looked from Jean to Everton. Their silence encouraged her, and she continued.

"Thousands of years ago the Sami people asked the gods for wisdom. Sami have a father god. We call him Radien Attje, which means 'powerful father.' The Norse people call this god Odin. They are probably the same god. They are probably even the same as the Christian god. He, or she these days, doesn't mind if different people give him, or her, a different name, or even a different gender. Sami believe that human souls descended from Radien Attje. Norse people believe that Odin is the father god who created all men. It's really the same idea.

"There is a good story about how Odin gained the knowledge of magic runes and true wisdom but how he paid a terrible and high price for these gifts. I'll tell you this story. It won't take long. It's really interesting. I have read a lot about it."

Sárá was up to speed in her story by now and did not need to check that her listeners were paying attention. Her brother, Oskár, drummed his fingers on the table silently, having heard this story many times, but otherwise everyone at the table was still.

"There was a world tree called Yggdrasil. It was a huge tree that sent roots out to all parts of the world. Odin actually had to hang himself from the world tree with a rope. I know it sounds terrible, doesn't it? He had to hang there for nine nights. Even though he was a god, he was injured in the side by a spear. He couldn't eat or drink. He was alone and in terrible pain. Just at the point where he was about to die, because gods can die, the secret of reading magic runes was revealed to him. Then his rope broke, and he fell from the tree. He had suffered terribly, but he now knew magic, and he had great power in the world. You might have spotted that this story is similar in some ways to the Christian story about suffering, crucifixion, and resurrection. This theme is quite common in god stories. It makes you wonder if the stories started from the same point, doesn't it?"

Sárá looked carefully at the two travellers, to check they understood this link and agreed with her. Neither Jean nor Everton moved. They were both waiting for the next part of the tale. Jean smiled and nodded slightly.

Sárá concluded that her audience remained engaged, smiled back at Jean, and resumed. "Now, Odin lived in a place called Asgard, the name for the home of all the Norse gods. Odin was the god of magic, prophecy, and wisdom. He did not like to stay in Asgard all the time. He was a curious god. Well, really, who would have wanted to stay at home all the time? That would be really boring, wouldn't it? And why would a god choose to be bored? That would be the god of boredom, I suppose. Anyway, he often came down to our world, which the Norse people called Midgard. He wandered around our world in a dark blue cloak with a silver clasp with magic runes engraved on it. These runes contained many magic spells. Odin was very good at disguises and often showed himself in different forms to humans. He might even be here in this room with us right now, and we would never know it. That is an exciting thought, isn't it? I often wonder if Odin is sneaking around following me and watching me. Odin also travelled on an eight-legged horse called Sleipnir, which sometimes pulled a sleigh. You can see the similarity to magic reindeer pulling a sleigh, and even to Father Christmas riding a magic sleigh. Except of course that reindeer don't have eight legs. People borrow stories from other people all the time. I think this is a good thing.

"Anyway, the story tells that Odin eventually became tired of too much travelling. Because travelling can be boring too. He thought of the idea that he could stay at home and rest more if he could see what was happening everywhere without travelling. Odin thought that if he had what he called true wisdom, he would be able to tell what was going on everywhere without travelling all the time.

"Now, in order to gain true wisdom, in those days, you had to drink from a magic well, which was in the land of the giants and guarded by a giant called Mimir. You see, there were no universities and schools where you could learn about calculus and poetry. These had not been invented at that time. Mimir had drunk from his well many times, so of course he was the wisest person in Midgard. The journey to Mimir's well was dangerous, with mountains to cross and blizzards of snow and ice. The magic well lay near the home of the giants, under a huge ash tree. As he rode along the road, Odin met a giant riding on a reindeer. Odin was disguised and had taken on the size of a giant, so the giant didn't recognise him. Odin said to the giant, 'There is something I would like to learn from you.'"

Tiny Sárá spoke the voice of Odin and the giant by lowering her tone as far as she possibly could. Although nine-year-old girls do not naturally have a deep or low voice, Sárá made a good effort at this, which added to the dramatic effect. Her audience appreciated her attempts to portray the voices of the king of the gods and a giant. Jean and Everton smiled at each other, enjoying this unexpected Sami virtuoso performance.

Sárá continued her story. "The giant replied, 'Ho ho ho. Before I can tell you anything, you must answer three riddles. If any of your answers are wrong, I will cut off your head. But if you answer all three correctly, you can ask me three questions, on the same terms. Do you agree?'

"Odin agreed to these terms. He had no choice if he wanted true wisdom, of course.

"'Well,' said the giant, 'these are the questions. What is the name of the river that divides Asgard from Jötunheim? What are the names of the horses that fly across the sky every day and night? And what is the name of the place where the last of all battles will be fought?'

"Odin breathed a sigh of relief. Thank goodness. He knew the answers. To him, these questions were easy. Actually, if you know the answer to any question, then it is easy by definition. 'Ifling is the deadly cold river that freezes in the instant any living thing falls into it. Skinfaxe and Hrimfaxe are the horses that dash day and night across the sky. The field for the last battle will be Vigard. That's where you and I are destined to fight at the end of all days,' said Odin.

"Odin was right, of course. The giant was very disappointed. Odin would be able to keep his head. The giant liked taking heads off and boiling them before eating them for dinner. But he was a good sport and followed the rules. 'Now it's your turn,' said the giant.

"Odin asked, 'What will be the last words that Odin will whisper into the ear of his son, Baldur?'

"'That's not a fair question,' said the giant. 'How could I possibly know that?'

"'Well,' said Odin, 'you didn't worry about being fair to me, did you? But don't worry; I don't actually want your head. You can keep it. Instead, just tell me what I'll have to give Mimir for a drink from the well of wisdom.'

"'He will ask for your right eye,' said the giant without pausing.

"Odin shuddered. 'That is a lot to ask for. Is there no other way?' he asked.

"'There is no other way if you want true wisdom,' said the giant. 'Many people have asked for the true wisdom from the well, but nobody has yet agreed to pay the price.'

"Odin nodded. He was glad to leave the wise but fierce giant and walk on. His path was hard, and there was a bitterly cold wind and rain, so his cloak was soon wet through. He fingered the clasp and whispered the magic runes. His cloak dried magically, and the weather improved. But the path was still rough, and he had to be very careful where he put his feet. Gods can trip over too, you know. Odin felt depressed, especially when he thought about the eye he would have to lose forever. He thought of the terrible pain he would suffer. When the gods were in Midgard, the land of men, they had to feel what men feel and suffer what men and women suffer. But Odin knew he would have to give up his eye to gain the wisdom he needed to help the world. I think that he would have been helped if Jean had been available to provide some talking therapy for him."

Sárá paused and looked up to smile at Jean. Jean smiled back and nodded in agreement. Everyone laughed in delight at this fusion of two worlds.

"Anyway, Odin continued his journey," said Sárá. "Eventually, after turning a sharp bend in the road, he was able to see the huge ash tree bordering Jötunheim, the giants' land. It was indeed a wonderful and beautiful tree, very tall and very deep rooted, as ash trees generally are. Its deep roots drew wisdom from the four corners of the earth. And near the tree, Mimir stood by his well. 'Ho there, Odin, I've been waiting for you,' said Mimir, because he had drunk from the well and knew everything that would happen and everyone's name before they told him. 'Are you thirsty?' said Mimir.

"'Yes,' said Odin. 'I have a great thirst for wisdom, and yes, Mimir, I need to drink from your well.'

"Mimir laughed. 'Many are thirsty for my waters, but they do not get to drink from them. No one has yet agreed to my price. You must give me your right eye if you want to drink.'

"Odin considered one last time if the price was too high. His pale blue eyes were the colour of the sky on a bright winter day, when the sun shines and frost is hard on the ground—very like my eyes, in fact. His eyes could pick out the tiniest bird miles and miles away across the frozen tundra. If a human, or even a god, looked him in the eyes, they felt a kind of awe. But in the end, he did have two eyes, so he could spare one. 'I will pay your price, Mimir,' he said, and he cut his right eye from his head.

"The pain was searing and terrible. He gave it to the guardian of the well. Mimir dropped the eye in his well. The eye remained in the well forever, seeing everything. Mimir handed Odin a horn brimming with the waters of wisdom. Odin took a deep drink. Immediately he saw everything that had happened and everything that was in the future. Wisdom flooded into him, and he saw more clearly with one eye than he had ever seen with two eyes. Most people don't want to know the future because some of it is not good news. But some people do and try to find it out, one way or another. Usually it does them no good. It is probably wise to keep away from fortune-tellers for a normal person. But Odin was not a normal person. He was a Norse god, and when he saw the joy that would come to him, he laughed with happiness. But seeing all the sorrows and troubles that would happen to humankind, he also knew what he could do to help. For even though the gods really have no need to trouble themselves about us mortals and our puny lives and petty sufferings, they do actually care, at least some of the time. After he drank from the well of true wisdom, he knew that he must never let evil get the upper hand in the world of humans. We mortals can be grateful for that small mercy.

"And that is the story of how Odin got his true wisdom and of how he lost his eye. It is also possible that that is how he got his name too, because Odin—or 'Odeen' in Russian—means the number one. Perhaps the Russians meant that he had just one eye.

"There is another tale about Mimir much later. It is quite shocking, especially for a nine-year-old girl. But I can cope," said Sárá, grinning widely. "After one of the many wars between the gods, Mimir's head was cut off and sent to Odin. Odin rubbed the head with magic herbs and chanted special spells over it, because he did not want to lose all of Mimir's wisdom. Soon Mimir's eyes opened, and his head spoke to Odin. Odin stored Mimir's head next to the magic well of knowledge so that he could consult Mimir for wisdom whenever it was needed."

Sárá paused again and took a small sip of water from her glass. But she was not yet finished entertaining her audience.

"That was fascinating, Sárá," said Jean. "You know a lot about these things. You must be a great reader."

"Yes, Jean. I read all the time. I love reading. Reading is like drinking from the well of wisdom, but I don't have to cut out one eye to do it," said Sárá.

Vulle and Ánne watched their young daughter holding court with the English tourists. This was something that they were clearly familiar with, but they smiled with pleasure.

"Now, weather is a very important feature of our lives in Norway," said Sárá. "You must understand that the weather is a matter of life and death for Sami reindeer herders. A sudden change of weather can be the difference between survival or perishing for a whole family. So understanding thunder, lightning, snow, and ice is very important to us. Sami have been trying to understand these things for thousands of years.

"In Sami, the thunder god is called Horgalles, also written as Thora Galles. This god is sometimes also called Tiermes. He is often depicted as a wooden figure with a nail or piece of flint in his head, and one or two hammers, and sometimes a Sami shaman drum. Horgalles is the god of thunder, lightning, rainbow, weather, oceans, and lakes. He punishes evil demons, or trolls, who live in the mountains. He destroys them with lightning, or shoots them with his bow, or dashes their brains out with his hammer."

Sárá brought her tiny hand down on the wooden bench with a small thump and smiled at the two tourists. Jean and Everton both smiled back, not daring to speak.

Sárá continued. "He can send thunder and lightning with one hammer and take it back with his other hammer. Some people think that the word Horgalles is borrowed from the old Norse

Þorr Karl, which means the 'Old Man Thor.' So you can see that the Norse god Thor is the same person as Horgalles. In one of our tales, the thunder god, who was ten pines high, was hunting a large magical white reindeer that had a black head, white body, silver coat, burning eyes, and golden horns. Horgalles was hunting with his dogs, which were the size of reindeer. He carried arrows in a sack on his back, and he lived in a rock crevice in the mountains. His bow was a rainbow. When he drew his bow and shot an arrow, the earth moved. He drove a cart, in which he had all his possessions. The devil chased after him, but he was good at running from the devil. As the cart moved, it caused thunder. This god was able to scare off fiends or trolls with his arrows.

"The hunt of Horgalles has been going on for thousands of years. We believe that when the hunter shoots his first arrow at the reindeer, the earth shakes. When he shoots his second arrow, the earth lights up in flames and mountains start boiling like water. When the dogs jump on the reindeer and tear it to pieces, the world will end.

"The Sami believed that thunder drinks water from rivers and lakes and later causes it to pour down as rain. So we understood that our crops depended on the thunder god in some way.

"There is also a golden horned spirit in Norse mythology. He is called Heimdall. You might have read about him. He is connected with rainbows and the *Bivrost*, the northern lights. We like to swap our gods with our Norse brothers and sisters. We are not a jealous people.

"Now, the hunter god tale is an attempt to explain various natural phenomena, including earthquakes, meteorites falling to earth, rain, lightning, and thunder, of course. It has similarities to end-of-the-world tales in many cultures, including Christian writings.

"You might know that the American Dr. Benjamin Franklin was the first person to deduce that lightning was really a current of some sort, flowing like water. Dr. Franklin was a great man who helped save many lives from the thunder god by inventing the lightning conductor. I hope I invent something as useful as this in my life. However, it might be said that he also caused the extinction of our thunder god by explaining thunder and lightning using his new science.

"Snow is also very important to us. It is so important that we have more than two hundred names for different types of it. This is something we share with the Inuit people. They, too, depend on an understanding of the nature of ice and snow for their safety. For example, *bajádat* is a type of snow that is hard enough to prevent our skis from sinking, *cáskat* is a type of snow into which our feet sink, making walking difficult, and *ceavvi* is hard snow that can support many people walking on it. The nature of snow is important for our safety."

"Wow. Such a lot of information. You are just full of information," said Jean. "Thank you for giving us such a useful introduction before our arctic safari trip."

Sárá took this as an invitation for more legends and stories. "Did you know there is a tale about a magical reindeer who can transform into a human?" she said.

"Mr. and Mrs. Everton will be with us for many days, Sárá," said Ánne. "You can tell more stories to them when we are relaxing in our cabins. There is no hurry. They will be with us for many days."

Sárá nodded to her mother but said nothing more.

"We look forward to hearing about the magical reindeer man," said Jean, smiling at Sárá.

After a few more minutes of small talk, the Issáksons finished their drinks and stood to leave.

"We will see you all again tomorrow. You will be travelling on the dogsleds with an American couple, Mr. and Mrs. Gibson. You will meet them tomorrow as well," said Vulle.

Sárá gave Jean a tight hug before the Issáksons left.

Lying in bed an hour later, Jean and Everton talked over the encounter.

"They seem a very pleasant family," said Everton.

"The little girl, Sárá, is very confident. She seems to take charge," said Jean.

"She certainly took a shine to you," said Everton.

"This is going to be a great trip. I can feel it in my bones," said Jean.

Chapter 2

Northern Lights

Jean and Everton awoke to a dark morning, every bit as dark as the previous day and evening. The lights of the city sparkled, just as they had the previous evening. Beyond the city lights, the world was still pitch black.

While they ate breakfast in the hotel, a large TV in the restaurant area was playing news. Once again, the newscaster was speaking in English, with intermittent forays into Norwegian. As they ate, Everton read the booklet provided by their tour company, and Jean listened to the world news.

"The newscaster is speculating that the illnesses in London and New York might be linked. I wonder if this might be a terrorist incident, attacking on two continents at once, a form of biological terrorism," said Jean.

A pile of newspapers was set out on a large table at the entrance to the restaurant. Jean walked over, picked out one English and one American newspaper, and returned to their breakfast table.

"They do think that these illnesses are both a similar type of infection," said Jean, after reading for several minutes.

After a brief pause, Everton looked up. "What was that?" he said.

"The news. There is a suspicion that the outbreaks of infection are linked," said Jean.

"OK. That sounds serious. The medical people are usually pretty good at this. I'm sure they will have it all under control," said Everton, and he looked back at his tour booklet.

Jean read for a few more minutes.

"The World Health Organization are saying they might have to recommend restricting travel if these infections are linked. What if we can't fly back to England after our trip? We could be trapped in a winter wonderland. For months. Or even for years," she said with a wide smile.

Everton was engrossed in his tour book and spoke without looking up. "I doubt that," he said. "They would probably deport us in handcuffs if we tried to stay that long."

Jean swapped her attention back to the TV news. "Did you know that Norway has a serious problem with suicide, hard drug abuse, and alcoholism? Apparently, the solitude of arctic life is causing some sort of public health crisis. We might be driven to drink and drugs by months of arctic quarantine," she said.

Everton looked up and appeared to be about to respond.

"Mmm," was all he said in the end.

"Well, I see no obvious signs of any of this epidemic of substance abuse and death in Tromsø," said Jean. "At first pass, it looks like a very clean, well-organised, affluent society, with polite, friendly, hardworking, and healthy people."

There was no response again from Everton, who continued to study his tour guide.

Jean gave up on informing Everton about international and current affairs and returned to the buffet bar for more cream for her coffee.

After breakfast, they returned to their room, donned their multiple layers of warm weather clothes again, and walked out to meet the instructors for their trip into the arctic wilderness.

The dark day was cold but calm, with no wind and no snow falling. A drop in temperature had brought a mist to the city.

"The invisible army of snow elves has cleared the pavement of most of the snow that fell overnight. How do they do that? And why can't we do the same in England?" said Jean.

Her question remained unanswered.

Snow was heaped in thick piles in the gutters. They crunched over the piles and through the dry snow in their thick boots, linking arms to reduce the risk of falling on the icy patches of road. Road traffic continued normally despite the conditions. The brightly lit offices and shops were already teeming with people.

They entered the lobby of a small hotel on the dockside, where they were to meet the instructor for their trip out to the frozen mountains of northern Norway and Finland.

A group of tourists had already gathered in the hotel reception area. They all waited patiently, whispering to their partners or friends and cautiously eyeing up their fellow travellers.

Just after 10:00 a.m., a neatly dressed lady with short blond hair walked through the hotel main doors and stamped the snow off her boots. "Travellers with Nordic Journeys, please follow me," she said, looking at the group of tourists.

The lobby emptied as the entire assembled group followed the lady into a conference room. Chairs were arranged in rows, with a flip chart, whiteboard, and a table, on which hot and cold drinks were set out.

The tour guide stood at the front of the room. "Good morning, everyone. I am Margarét Gudmundsdóttir. I am pleased to meet you all, and I welcome you to your Nordic journey. Please help yourselves to a drink and then a seat," she said.

A few minutes later the group of tourists were obediently sitting facing Margarét.

"You will all be sharing a journey of a lifetime over the next few nights and days. You will all be friends for an exciting arctic safari. I suggest we each introduce ourselves and tell one another where we come from," said Margarét.

One by one, the tourists introduced themselves.

A large man stood up. "I am Henry Gibson, and this is my wife, Beth. We are from Florida, in the USA. We don't get any snow in Florida. This is our first time in the frozen north," he said. Beth smiled and waved to the people in the room.

A smaller man stood next. "My name is Rolf, and this is my wife, Ulva. We are from Germany," he said, indicating a small elderly lady with grey hair.

Jean stood next. "Hello, everyone. I am Jean Everton, and this is Kenneth Everton, my husband. You can call me Jean. People call my husband Everton. Confusing, I know. Don't ask me why. It's a long story."

A dark-haired man stood. "We are the Moretti family. We are looking forwards to seeing the lights," he said with a broad smile. His two children giggled and prodded each other.

Finally, a muscular young man stood up. "I am Christiaan, and I am travelling with Willem and Yvette. We are all from Holland. We don't have any mountains in Holland. We hope to see the northern lights every day and night in the mountains, since it is nighttime all of the time," he said, smiling broadly.

"Perfect. Thank you, everyone. I hope you see the aurora every day also, Christiaan," said Margarét. "I am sure you have all read the itinerary for the trip and the safety information, which we sent to you all. To summarize for you, this afternoon you will be driving up to the Halti Mountain area, to Camp Arktis, which is on the border of Finland and Norway. We hope you get a super view of the northern lights. Overnight, you will stay in chalets in the countryside at Camp Arktis. Tomorrow you will travel to Camp Trollfjell. Some of you will be travelling on dogsleds, which should be very exciting, and some of you will be taking snowmobile rides by a different route. Those who take the dogsleds will be looked after by Vulle Issákson and his family. They are a Sami family, and they will be your guides for the rest of your trip. Camp Trollfjell is a Sami camp, with cabins and *lavvu*, a type of tent. You will be there for several nights over Christmas. The lavvu are the tents used by the Sami in the arctic. Very warm inside. For those who have chosen the snowmobile route, your guide will be Edo, who will also be driving your minibus today.

"Now, it is very important that you remember that you will be out of contact for several days while you are travelling in the mountains and staying with the Sami or in Camp Arktis and Camp Trollfjell. Your mobile devices will not work out in the countryside very well, if at all. You will be at least fifty kilometres from Tromsø or more. Your instructors and Sami guides can use satellite phones for emergencies, but access for emergency services in the countryside can sometimes be difficult if the weather causes problems. At the moment, the weather is looking good, but this can change quickly in Norway. Our roads are cleared often. We have the best snow ploughs in the world. But if the snow comes down hard, the roads can be blocked for a few days. You have already filled in your medical questionnaires, so I don't think there will be any problems. Remember our temperatures here in Norway can fall as low as thirty below Celsius, which is minus twenty-two Fahrenheit for our American cousins. So your clothing is very important. Always put on your warm clothes, in multiple layers, when outside, even if only for a few minutes. Keep your hands, feet, head, and noses warm at all times."

Margarét looked at the assembled tourists and paused. The silence allowed the warning to sink in. Nobody spoke for half a minute.

Jean and Everton glanced at each other and smiled in anticipation at the journey before them.

"Margarét seems like a very strict primary schoolteacher. Very stern and serious. You had better behave yourself," Jean whispered to Everton.

Margarét explained more details of the excursion to the assembled group and then asked them to meet again with their luggage the same evening outside the hotel, to drive out to the countryside and chase the northern lights.

"We have seen news of the infection outbreak in New York and London," said the American lady, Beth. "We just flew in from Florida, via New York. They are talking about travel restrictions. What are the plans in the event of travel problems?"

"Thank you, Beth," said Margarét. "A good question. At present, there are no travel restrictions. We don't think there will be any. Norway is not affected at all by New York or London health problems. However, if your travelling is interrupted, you all have insurance, and you will be able to claim, of course. In Norway, we are not normally affected by travel problems in central Europe or North America."

The young man, Christiaan, stood and spoke. "My friends and I are interested in using the snowmobiles from Camp Trollfjell to explore your beautiful wilderness. Will we be permitted to take snowmobiles out on our own and enjoy the natural beauty of Norway?"

"We are asked about this quite often," said Margarét. "As long as you are experienced using a snowmobile and you have navigation skills, then the Sami experts will be happy to let you explore on your own. There are dangers in the Norwegian wilderness of course. We have large predators. And we must all respect the weather, which can change very quickly. The Sami leaders will assess your skills once you are at the camp."

Christiaan turned to his two friends, and they exchanged high fives. Christiaan muttered something in Dutch as he sat.

"You understand Dutch," whispered Everton to Jean. "What did he just say?"

"I think it was 'I told you so,'" said Jean quietly.

Jean and Everton walked back through the freezing snow to their hotel to collect their luggage. Before leaving for their northern lights trip, they visited the hotel restaurant for lunch. The Norwegian newscaster was again speaking in English about the outbreaks of infection.

"They are still going on about these people with infection," said Jean. "It looks as if a couple of them in London have died. The World Health Organization has become involved. At present, they are saying there is no cause for alarm."

"That sounds reassuring. I doubt it will make any difference to us. I'm sure the medical services are doing their best. It's probably a good time to be away from the usual media hysteria in England," said Everton.

Jean continued to watch the Norwegian news for a couple of minutes.

After the meal, they packed their spare cold weather clothes in backpacks and made their way to the meeting point to catch the minibus into the countryside.

The bus was already waiting for them. Before the journey, they were ushered into an adjoining office building, and each was provided with an insulated full bodysuit to wear over their own clothing. Once they were zipped into their new clothing, Jean and Everton settled into two of the minibus seats, behind the American couple, Henry and Beth. They felt like gigantic, well-insulated Michelin men.

Beth turned to them. "Hi, Jean. We are very excited to be going out to see the lights," she said. "Let's hope we get a great display."

"Yes indeed. I think the omens are good. We saw the aurora yesterday in the middle of the city, while we were shopping," said Jean.

"Wow. You were lucky," said Beth. "I do a bit of painting, back in Florida. I am hoping to get some inspiration from the aurora for my painting."

"She is just being modest," said Henry. "Beth is a fantastic painter. She sells hundreds of paintings in the US. Our house is like an art gallery."

Beth's cheeks flushed a little, and she changed the subject. "Did you see the news about the infection outbreak in New York and London? We just heard that the US and UK governments have announced that they think that the two outbreaks are linked. Some form of Ebola has gotten into our countries somehow. They are talking about possible travel bans to and from some countries. It sounds worrying," said Beth.

"Calm down, Beth. It'll all blow over," said Henry, patting Beth on the knee. "Ebola is not something we need to worry about. It's a disease that affects poor, hot countries. Norway is a rich, cold country."

Vulle Issákson climbed into the minibus, followed by another man. Vulle wore his fox-fur hat with large earflaps, similar to Everton's. Over the top of a fur coat, he was wearing a large, dark, woollen hooded cape covering the top half of his body. He raised his large hands.

"Hello, everyone. I am Vulle Issákson. You can call me Vulle. I am your guide for tonight, and for some of you for the next five days. This is Edo, our driver. Edo will be driving us into the hills tonight and will be helping some of you with snowmobiles tomorrow. You will be meeting my family this evening at Camp Arktis. This afternoon we will be going into the mountains, where it will be very cold. When we get out to see the lights, keep your gloves on and your clothes fastened. We don't want your fingers, toes, or noses to get too cold. Let me know if you need anything. We have hot drinks whenever you want them."

Vulle walked down the minibus. As he passed Everton, he noticed the hat, which Everton held in his lap. "You have a special hat, Mr. Everton. I have a very similar hat. We will both have warm ears in the mountains," he said.

"I just bought it yesterday in Tromsø," said Everton. "Fox fur. Looking forwards to using it."

"My wife, Ánne, made mine from animals that I had hunted. It's the best hat I ever had. And the warmest," said Vulle.

The road journey to the Halti Mountain area took a couple of hours. The Norwegian countryside was blanketed in snow as they drove through it, but the permanent darkness meant they could not see far into the countryside. The warm orange glow of house lights peeked out from windows as they passed an occasional house or cabin. As they drove farther from Tromsø, they steadily climbed into the hills. For a few miles, there were fewer houses, then dark pine forest, and finally open countryside covered in deep snow.

Vulle spoke to them intermittently to point out places of interest and to explain historical facts about Norway and the Sami people. The road they took passed into Finland and then back into Norway again, without any border controls or any recognisable change in the road.

"The Sami people live in Norway, Sweden, Finland, and Russia," said Vulle at one point, with a broad smile. "We call the lands where the Sami people have traditionally lived Sápmi. We pass between all four countries with our reindeer, moving from summer to winter feeding grounds. The borders don't apply to us or to the reindeer. We were here for thousands of years before the borders, and we will probably be here long after the borders disappear."

After several hours' driving, Edo stopped the minibus in a siding on a section of road between two hills. They were already high in the mountains, and the peaks were only a few hundred feet above them. There were no trees, just deep snow in every direction.

"We are stopping in this mountain pass for about an hour. It will give us a wonderful view of the sky in the darkness without any light pollution. Hopefully the aurora will visit us here," said

Vulle. "You can see Halti Mountain just over there to the east. And to the northwest, you can just see the lights of the coast and Tromsø. It is more than fifty kilometres away. We will get out here to take a look at the sky. Put on your double gloves, and keep your clothes fastened. It is more than twenty degrees below zero outside. We will be coming back for hot drinks after our walk."

The tourists all alighted from the minibus. Edo joined them, and Vulle then led them north into the snow, towards one of the nearby mountain peaks. As they walked, quite suddenly, ribbons of coloured light appeared over their heads and started weaving and rippling across the sky. Green, blue, and pink light waves combined and separated across hundreds of kilometres of sky above them.

"Wow. Look at that. Fantastic," said Christiaan, one of the young Dutch travellers.

There were appropriate gasps of astonishment from the tourists.

They walked uphill slowly for about ten minutes before reaching the peak. The lights continued to flow above their heads. Vulle stopped them, and they stood staring up at the sky. Pink, green, yellow, and blue flashed into existence, then combined and danced above them. The display had lasted for more than twenty minutes, stretching from horizon to horizon.

They were all gasping in delight. Even Vulle was pleased.

"This is really spectacular tonight," said Vulle. "You can see that I have arranged a special display for you, of course. Only VIP visitors get to see the aurora like this."

There was a faint groan from someone of the group. Beth was standing over Henry, who was kneeling in the snow.

"Henry isn't feeling so well, Vulle," said Beth. "I think we'd better go back to the bus."

Vulle knelt next to Henry and asked a few questions in a quiet voice. Henry nodded. Vulle helped Henry to stand. As Henry reached a standing position, he suddenly became limp, sagged, and dropped face-first into the snow with a dull thud. Vulle immediately rolled Henry onto his back, shook his shoulder several times, and called his name. There was no response from Henry. Vulle listened closely to Henry's mouth for any breathing.

"He is breathing. We need to get him back to the warm minibus. Stay with him, and I will get a stretcher," said Vulle. His voice was calm, but there was a serious edge to it.

Within a few minutes, Vulle was back from the minibus with a stretcher. Everton and Edo helped Vulle roll Henry into the stretcher and then strap him to it. The three Dutch youngsters helped Vulle and Edo carry Henry down the hill to the minibus. Beth followed, linking arms with Jean. The Italians followed in a group, chatting furiously in Italian. The German couple walked at the rear. Henry started grunting and moving as they carried him.

"You are all right, Henry. You fainted, and we are taking you back to the minibus to warm up. You will feel much better very soon," said Vulle.

Henry looked surprised and stared up at the northern lights, twinkling and flashing above them, but he remained silent.

Once they were back in the minibus, Edo started the engine to warm things up, and Vulle poured warm drinks for Henry and the other tourists. Within ten minutes, Henry was sitting up, smiling and talking, and sipping hot tea as if nothing had happened.

"I feel great now. Not sure what happened out there. So sorry I spoiled your northern lights, folks," said Henry.

"Not at all, Henry. I am just happy you are OK," said Vulle, smiling at Henry. "We don't like losing clients in the hills. Bad for morale. We did get a great display of the aurora. I hope you saw it and will remember it."

"In truth, I can't remember much after we left the vehicle, Vulle," said Henry. "It's all a blur."

After ten more minutes of warming up, Henry was happy to continue. They drove farther east into the hills for half an hour, descending slightly, and entered a forest area with tall pines. After several miles driving through the forest, which provided a dense and dark avenue either side of the single-lane road, they stopped in a clearing. There were wooden cabins, some of which looked like tents, dotted around the clearing. The largest cabin, built to look like a large tent, stood in the centre, with a warm glow shining out from its windows. Lights above the door of each cabin pushed back the darkness in small pools.

Behind the cabins, in a cleared area, were a group of small wooden kennels mounted off the ground on wooden legs. A dog was chained to each kennel. As they arrived, the dogs jumped out of their kennels and started to leap around and bark enthusiastically, straining at their chains. A large wooden shed stood next to the kennels.

"We will show you to your cabins soon. This is where we will meet and eat," said Vulle, pointing to the larger tentlike building. "But first we can meet the dogs."

Vulle walked to the dogs and greeted each of them warmly. The dogs were clearly very excited to see Vulle, and they jumped up, placing their front paws on his chest to greet him. The tourists stood around admiring the energy of the dogs in temperatures so far below freezing.

"They think we might go out tonight," said Vulle. "They always want to run. Run, run, run. They just love to run. You can say hello to them. They are very friendly."

Vulle encouraged the tourists to make friends with his dogs.

As they fussed over the dogs, Jean turned to Everton. "They have different-coloured coats, but most of their eyes are such a bright blue colour," she said.

"Yes. Slightly spooky seeing dogs with such light-coloured eyes. It feels as if they are looking through me," said Everton.

The dogs gradually settled and started jumping into their kennels, curling up in straw bedding to keep warm. They seemed to realise that they would not be getting a run that day.

Vulle and Edo showed each group to their cabin, explained how to use the heaters and showers, and gave some instructions for dinner. Henry was feeling well again after the warm drive and drinks, and he thanked Vulle and the others for their help.

The tourists all congregated in the larger meeting cabin for their evening meal around 7:00 p.m. Vulle's wife, Ánne, had prepared roast reindeer for dinner. Vulle introduced his family to the wider group of travellers, and the children, Sárá and Oskár, helped to serve the visitors. Henry and Beth both ate well. It appeared that Henry had fully recovered.

Vulle's family sat with Jean and Everton. As they finished their meal, the rest of the guests had already left the dining cabin for the night. Jean and Everton were left, with Vulle and his family and Edo. Ánne, Oskár, and Edo started to clear away the crockery. Vulle brought a bottle of spirits to the table, where Sárá still sat with Jean and Everton.

"This gin is made from glacier water, melted in the Norwegian Lyngen Alps, near Tromsø. It is called Bivrost gin. You probably already know that the Bivrost is a magical bridge between heaven and earth. Some people believe that the northern lights are the Bivrost. I recommend a small glass of this before bedtime. It will help you dream of magical things," said Vulle.

"How could we resist," said Everton.

Vulle poured a small glass each for Jean, Everton, and himself.

"Vulle, the lights were fantastic. Thank you so much for the tour. And thank you for your help for Henry. He seems fine now," said Jean.

"Ja. I hope he remains well for our sled trip tomorrow," said Vulle. "If he becomes ill again, I will need to take him back to the city."

"I noticed you were wearing a cape when we were out in the cold countryside," said Everton. "This is very different to our thick parka jackets. It looks a bit like a Mexican poncho. I am surprised you are warm enough in the cape, at more than twenty below zero."

Vulle smiled at the Englishman. "You would be very surprised if you wore it. The cape we call a Luhkka. It is made from thick wool. We call the wool *wadmal*." Vulle smiled. "It has magical qualities. Much better than modern cloth. It is much warmer than most coats. It stores the heat, which rises within it. When the weather is really cold, we wear it over a fur coat, called a *beaska*. Today was not really cold, of course. Just a mild winter night," said Vulle.

The cabin was lit with candles, which flickered shadows on the walls and ceiling. A wood fire in the centre of the cabin emitted an orange glow around, ensuring that it was comfortable and warm for the tourists.

"How long have the Sami been living so far north?" said Jean.

"Thousands of years we have been here. Since long before the Romans invaded Britain," said Sárá.

"Do they teach you about Romans invading Britain in school?" said Jean.

"Yes. And I have read about it too. The Romans could not get so far north as this. They preferred the warmth of Italy. They didn't even like the cold of northern Scotland. They built two walls to keep out the savages in Scotland. Did you know that?" said Sárá.

The nine-year-old Sárá appeared to be giving a lesson in British and Scandinavian history to the British tourists.

"Would you like to hear a little about the legends of the origins of the Sami people?" said Sárá.

"That would be wonderful, Sárá. Tell us all about it," said Jean.

"I will tell you about Meandash, the reindeer man. He is an important part of the Sami world," said Sárá.

"One day, many thousands of years ago, there was a land unknown to mortal Sami people. By a strange coincidence, this unknown land was very similar in appearance to the Kola peninsula, in which reindeer lived, which is now part of Russia. This land had existed since the beginning of time. The tundra and reindeer also existed at the beginning of time, before men came to the land. This land of magical reindeer was separated from the land of Sami mortals by a wide and magic river of blood, called the Meandash River. The river had waves of lungs and stones of liver, because it was really a living creature. It just looked like a river. The river separated all Sami kinfolk but also linked them by blood. I think this is called a metaphor."

Nine-year-old Sárá looked at Jean and then Everton to check whether they needed an explanation of what a metaphor was. Suitably reassured by their expressions, she continued. "An old Sami man and his wife who lived in those days had three daughters. These daughters received proposals of marriage from a raven, a seal, and a reindeer, all of which could take human form. This might seem strange to us today, but it was not such a strange thing for those magical times. These animals in the story represented the sky, the water, and the earth. You might have noticed this since one can fly, one can swim, and one walks on the land.

"The raven married the oldest daughter, and the seal married the middle daughter. The reindeer and the youngest daughter are important at a later stage of this story. The old man and his wife took turns visiting their married daughters. The raven and the seal both set up their homes near a sea cliff.

"The old man and woman did not like the raven family, its bare living place in dried pine trees, its untidiness, and the strange diet of odds and ends, tripe, and its habit of eating heads. The raven also pecked out one of his wife's eyes and crippled her. Despite this, they had many raven children. This is surprising, really, but wives in those days did not have our modern laws. They were obviously very tolerant of grumpy husbands, and this family was very fertile, despite their abusive relationship. They would have been referred to our social services, and the children might have been taken into state care these days, of course.

"The old man and woman found that the seal was not a good husband to their second daughter. The seal had bitten off one of their daughter's hands, which is again surprising to us in modern times, of course. The old man and woman did not like the vast emptiness of the ocean, which they found to be a lonely place, becoming dirty with seal blubber, or the fishy diet. They thought that the seal was too rough with their daughter. This is understandable, since it had bitten off her hand.

"The older two of the three daughters were also evil and disobedient people. They stole from their parents. In due course, they were both gored to death by a reindeer and then turned into lifeless stones. The lesson is that such women were not fit to become the ancestors of the reindeer people. This part of the story is an encouragement to all daughters to be obedient to their parents. As a daughter myself, I am not sure about this part. My mummy and daddy are very kind to me, and I want to obey them because I trust them. But if they were unkind to me, I am not sure if I would feel the same way. So this part of the story also helps us to consider the rights and wrongs of being a parent and how to behave as a daughter."

Sárá paused and looked at her mother and father. They both smiled back and nodded to her reassuringly.

She continued. "The youngest daughter was very wise. She was capable of making contact between different parts of the universe. She was able to chant. While chanting, she chewed alder bark and spat this into the river. This is a bit like making magic spells. Remember that the world then was full of magic spells. She chanted the river of blood into drying up. In this way, she was able to cross the river of blood.

"The youngest daughter is sometimes called the Meandash-maiden because she crossed the Meandash River. She had human form on one side of the river and reindeer form on the other side, which is a very useful trick if you live in the north. She lived among the reindeer sometimes when in the reindeer land, but at other times, she lived in a tent. Her tent was made from reindeer bones. She especially loved the reindeer calves and tied red ribbons to their ears, which were crocheted by her mother, to mark them as her kin. I think this part of the story tells us that the Sami felt very close to the reindeer, which helped them to survive so far north. They thought of reindeer almost like brothers and sisters. Without the reindeer, it is unlikely that the Sami would have moved away from the coast, where we caught fish, and into the forests and mountains.

"Now I must tell you that the Sami believe that the bones contain the soul, because the bones are preserved longest after we die. Of course, we now know that our DNA is preserved best in bones for a very long time. We can take DNA from mammoth skeletons that are millions of years old. So the origin of this soul belief, or theory, has a basis in truth. Sami observations about bones were accurate after all, despite their lack of knowledge about biochemistry. They believed the evidence of their senses and made quite good deductions. Anyway, I am drifting away from my story, but I think this is interesting.

"While the daughter who was the Meandash-maiden was in human form, and while she was still a virgin, a reindeer herd approached her tent one day and encircled it. She took the shape of a reindeer cow and flirted with the dominant reindeer. He rode around her tent three times. This was a traditional way to propose marriage to her in those days. The reindeer used one door to enter her tent, and she used another door. As you might have guessed—and it is quite normal in this type of story—she fell pregnant. They set up their home near a forest lake. A reindeer baby was born, followed by more reindeer children. There is much more very interesting detail about her courtship, of course, but I am condensing this for you this evening. I can tell you more at another time if you are interested."

Sárá took a sip from her glass of water. Jean and Everton both sipped their Bivrost gin in response. The storyteller held her audience spellbound. Perhaps if there really was magic in Sápmi that evening, this was it.

"She named her eldest reindeer son Meandash. Meandash grew strong and healthy and soon started helping his mother collect firewood. You will have guessed that he could take the form of a man, with arms and hands, when he wanted to. This was how he collected firewood, of course. He could also talk like humans. Meandash did not feed on lichen and grass, like other reindeer, but instead went hunting, following the traditional life of ancient Sami. He had very good abilities to perform hard labour. His qualities convinced his tribe that they lived in an amazing time, before the universe was created and organised as it is now.

"This part of the story is describing some blood relationship between the reindeer and humans. A genetic relationship between reindeer and humans is now accepted, of course. Mr. Darwin from England explained this to us in his theory of evolution. He tells us that all forms of life share a common ancestor. We even share a common ancestor with lichen, and pine trees, wolves, eagles, and whales. So you see that the Sami had some idea of this tree of life thousands of years ago in their folklore. At least that is what I think. They were asking the same questions we do and finding similar answers, just with slightly less technology to help them.

"Back to the old man and his wife. They visited their youngest daughter. They were offered the best seats, covered in fur, because they were honoured guests. They had a grandson who was able to transform into human form. They found that the reindeer were clean animals that cared for their appearance and their blood. So they decided to settle among the reindeer with his wife.

"When Meandash grew into an adult, he became curious about his father and decided to find out whether he was man or reindeer. His mother warned him that this might be a dangerous journey for him. Meandash wet the bed when he was young, which is a serious problem in Sami culture, because it causes a bad smell, which can be detected by predators. Sami have to keep their tents very clean to avoid this danger. Meandash did a strange thing. He cut down a tree and wedged his mother's leg between wooden blocks. He then left his mother trapped by the wooden blocks and set off to the *fjeld*, which is a barren, rocky plateau, to explore the world. This part of the story explains why reindeer do not live with humans anymore. It might also be a growing-up story about how we all have to grow up and leave our parents at one time, to explore the world. Anyway, I think he was a little unkind to his mother, wedging her legs in the tree blocks. He could have just said goodbye to her and told her he would be back soon. I won't be like this to my mummy when I leave home."

Sárá looked at Ánne and shook her head. Ánne smiled back and shook her head also.

"During his travels, Meandash did many wonderful things. He gave men the hunting bow and taught them to hunt. He taught men that we must kill only one reindeer cow to feed our family. And he taught us that our reindeer will be smaller if we are disobedient to him. These rules were especially important for the reindeer that led the herds. These leader reindeer were sometimes Sami shaman who had transformed into reindeer, so they wanted to avoid being killed for food. I can understand this, of course. Being killed for food by accident is not a good thing.

"In this story, even though it was in ancient times, Sami understood that too much hunting was a bad thing. So hunting sustainably and conservation of natural resources were a part of Sami culture thousands of years ago. This is the tale of Meandash the reindeer."

Sárá paused and smiled at Jean and Everton.

"Phew. What a story. Thank you so much for telling this," said Jean.

"Some versions of this story have the youngest daughter marrying a dog-man, or a wolf-man, and having children who can alternate between human and wolf form," said Ánne. "There are multiple different versions of the tale in Finland, Russia, Sweden, and Norway. There are also echoes of this story in creation stories or ancestor legends in Christian literature too."

"I can see from this origin story how important reindeer are to the Sami, and ravens, seal, and wolves," said Jean.

It was late evening.

"Thank you again, Sárá, for your excellent story. We learned such a lot from you," said Jean.

"You are very welcome, Jean," said Sárá. "I will tell you more about the Sami when we have time."

As they all headed off to their cabins for the night, Vulle wished them all a good night's sleep. Vulle then walked up a small track, followed by his family and Edo, disappearing into the darkness of the surrounding forest.

Once they were in bed, Jean turned to Everton. "What a treat that was. A Sami reindeer legend, told by a nine-year-old. That girl will go far," said Jean.

"Quite amazing. I was captivated by the tale. I think Vulle and Ánne are both very proud to have such a clever little girl," said Everton.

CHAPTER 3

Dogs

EVERTON AND JEAN AWOKE to a blizzard swirling outside their cabin.

When they had arrived at Camp Arktis, the snow was already several feet deep off the roads. Silently overnight it had more than doubled in depth. The minibus was almost lost in a mountain of fresh snow. Among the cabins, lights cast a yellow glow. Farther out from the camp lights, the darkness was intense. The surrounding forest was inky black, even darker than the sky above.

Jean and Everton dressed warmly, even though it was only ten paces to the dining cabin. The deep snow made walking difficult. They linked arms and staggered through new snow, waist deep, to get to breakfast.

They stamped the snow off their boots as they entered the breakfast chalet. Hot food was already steaming on a buffet table. Most of the travellers were already sitting eating at wooden bench tables. They helped themselves to hot food and coffee and joined the group.

Vulle's family and Edo attended to the breakfast buffet, replenishing food and topping up the hot drinks.

As the last guest finished breakfast, Vulle stood and addressed the assembled tourists. "Good morning, everyone. I hope you are enjoying our fresh snow," said Vulle.

There was a general murmur of approval from the assembled travellers.

"The snow is deep, but it will not affect our travelling plans. Our sleds are designed to travel in this weather. Our dogs are very strong. Those of you who are travelling by dogsled will be warm and happy. I can see this. Also, those using snowmobiles will have some good fun today.

"My family are all experienced travellers. My children are young, but they know how to manage the dogs and sleds. They will be helping some of you to drive your sleds and get to Camp Trollfjell."

The Issáksons waved and smiled at the guests.

"We all speak English, but you can practice your Norwegian or your Sami with us too, if you want," said Vulle. "Edo will be looking after those of you who are taking the snowmobiles. Edo will show you how to use the machines. The heavy snow overnight has closed some roads in the mountains. At present, the roads across the countryside from Tromsø to Camp Arktis are closed, so we got through just in time. I am sure the ploughs will have the roads cleared in time for our return journey in a few days. The snowmobiles will be taking a different route to the dogs to Camp Trollfjell, and we will all meet up there this evening."

Vulle and his family started to clear away the breakfast tables.

Rolf, the small, elderly German, and his wife were sitting close to Jean and Everton. Rolf leaned over and spoke. "How are you liking the arctic conditions?"

"The wilderness around us looks spectacular, even in the arctic darkness," said Jean. "We are hoping to see more northern lights. We had a fabulous display during our journey here."

"Ja. We hope so also," said Rolf. "We have been to Scandinavia before, but we have never seen the aurora. Might I ask what you do for a living, Mrs. Everton?"

"I am a clinical psychologist, Rolf. Call me Jean please."

"Excellent, Jean," said Rolf. "I am retired now. I was professor of mathematics at Karlsruhe Institute of Technology. You have children?"

"Sadly no children," said Jean. "And you, Rolf?"

"We, too, have no children. My students were my children for many years."

Rolf turned to his wife, and she placed her hand softly over his on the table. They gazed at each other without speaking for a few seconds.

At that moment, Vulle walked past their table carrying some crockery. Rolf said, "Vulle, have you heard any news on the infection outbreak in London and New York?"

"Yes. I did hear something this morning. I believe that some travel restrictions have been imposed on some countries travelling into London and New York. There have been a couple of deaths in New York. It doesn't affect us in Norway at all. We can still travel freely within Norway. Flights from Norway to other European countries and the US are not affected. It is mainly China and African countries that are affected," said Vulle.

As the guests started filing out of the dining cabin, Vulle approached Henry, who was standing with Beth, Jean, and Everton.

"How are you feeling this morning, Henry?" said Vulle.

"Perfect. Not a problem overnight," said Henry, patting himself on the chest. "Fit as a fiddle. I am ready for anything today. Apologies to everyone for my minor problem last night."

"This is not a problem, Henry. I am just happy you have recovered," said Vulle. "Remember, we are all staying in the mountains for the next three nights. It will be very cold, all the time. Henry, Beth, Jean, and Mr. Everton, you are taking the sleds, and you must take all your spare warm clothes in your packs. Wear your full layers of thermal clothes outside always. Double gloves, double socks, warm hats, and neck and face coverings as well. We will be getting the dogs ready, and we hope to leave in an hour," said Vulle.

The travellers dispersed to their chalets and packed for their various journeys.

Once they were packed, Jean sat on the bed in their chalet. "What do you think about Henry? Did he look OK to you?" she said.

"I'm not sure," said Everton. "He is very overweight and a very big man. I wouldn't like to have to evacuate him in a medical emergency, from the back of beyond, by dogsled, in the arctic, in a blizzard. He says he is fine, but he looks a little grey round the gills to me. Having come this far, from Florida, he is clearly keen to get out and enjoy the trip. I don't really blame him for that."

"My thoughts entirely. I suppose it isn't our responsibility. Vulle and his family seem very experienced and confident. I suppose they have dealt with medical problems in the past," said Jean.

An hour later the four sled-travelling tourists were assembled behind the cabins, where the dogs were barking in excitement.

Vulle's family all wore sealskin boots, fur coats, fur hats, and thick fur gloves. Vulle wore his large woven cape over the top of his furs. Sárá was the smallest member of the family and had the appearance of a round and furry ball as she expertly harnessed the dogs to her sled. Vulle, Ánne, and the two Sami children showed the tourists how to harness the dogs to four large dogsleds. The dogs clearly knew they were going out for a run and were delighted. Those that had not yet been hitched to the sleds were jumping and straining against their chains. Jean, Everton, Beth, and Henry tried to help with the harnessing but managed to get tangled with the dogs and the harnesses. Vulle and his family patiently untangled the dogs from the tourists.

The rest of the travellers were gathered outside the wooden shed, where Edo was showing them the snowmobiles.

"Look at their bright blue eyes. They seem so piercing. As if they can see through me," said Jean, rubbing the head of a friendly white-and-grey husky who nuzzled against her leg.

"Beautiful. I agree. And they seem so lean for such cold weather," said Everton. "Not a scrap of excess fat on them. Their fur must be fantastic insulation. A bit like my beautiful new hat."

Jean and Everton were dressed in layers. Thermal under-clothes, warm shirts, undertrousers, waterproof and windproof over trousers and jackets, heavily insulated parka coats, with large hoods, neck and face warmers, inner gloves, and outer gloves. And of course, Everton wore his fox-fur hat proudly. Jean had a cotton hat topped with a black fox-fur bobble. Over their other clothing, they also wore the insulated one-piece whole bodysuits, which they had used the previous night for their mountain trip to see the lights.

"The snow has stopped falling, so the temperature has dropped," said Vulle to the four tourists travelling by sled. "It is heading to more than twenty below today. Here are some head torches to wear while we travel." He handed out small lights mounted on straps to be worn around the forehead. It was still pitch black outside the cabin lights, despite being close to mid-day. Various tracks disappeared into the dark forest in several directions.

"For the first couple of hours, Ánne, Oskár, Sárá, and I will be controlling the sleds," said Vulle. "You will all get a turn to drive if you want it. After crossing the frozen lake, we will be heading into the mountains, heading uphill to a mountain pass. Camp Trollfjell is on a plateau on the far side of these mountains. We will stop every hour or two. We will have some hot drinks for you if you want them. With luck, we will be at Camp Trollfjell by late afternoon. I will run through the basic sled instructions now and then remind you when we are ready to swap over."

As they put on their head torches, the lights shone on the snow and into the forest as they turned their heads. With the temperature so low, every speck of water was crystalline. A trillion glittering crystals reflected back their torch lights.

The backpacks containing their spare clothing, sleeping bags, and supplies were packed into waterproof bags and strapped onto the sleds.

"We might see some animals while we are travelling. We might also hear wolves. Don't worry, they will avoid us. They don't usually like us. We might see a fox or bear too if we are lucky, but this is rare. Bears should be hibernating by this time of year," said Vulle.

Each sled was large enough for a driver and a passenger, to-gether with a bag of luggage or provisions. Vulle and Oskár also stowed a rifle each, in a waterproof case, on their sleds. Oskár took the front sled, and Vulle took the rear sled. Eight dogs were hitched to each sled. By now, the dogs were whining, barking, and straining at their collars and leads. They clearly couldn't understand why the humans were delaying their run.

Jean, Everton, Henry, and Beth were each seated on one of four sleds, while Oskár and Sárá carefully covered the tourists' legs with thick blankets made from reindeer hide.

"This will keep you cosy and warm, Jean," said Sárá, tucking in Jean's blanket.

"I am warm already, but you are very kind. Thank you so much, Sárá," said Jean.

When the sleds were ready, the Issákson family stood on the footboard of one sled each. Oskár took the lead sled, and Vulle took the back sled, with Sárá and Ánne driving the middle two sleds.

With a shout from Vulle, the claw brakes were released, and the dogs leaped into action. The four sleds shot along the trail heading east into the forest.

The sleds followed deep tracks that were still visible in the snow despite the recent new snowfall. The dogs knew the route, with few instructions from Vulle or his family. The two children handled their dogs confidently, speeding up or slowing down, leaning left or right without hesitation or instruction from their parents.

There was little wind in the first hour of travel. Cold air flowed over the faces of the travellers. Their head torches illuminated innumerable tiny crystals covering almost every part of the landscape. As they passed along the track, through the forest, they crossed small streams without pausing, the dogs easily leaping across and the sleds spanning the gap without difficulty. The trees gradually thinned, and they emerged into a large flat plain between mountains. A frozen lake lay beneath them. Patches of dry snow dotted the plain of blue ice. The scale of the countryside switched from close and intimate to majestic and breathtaking. Under their triple layers of warm clothing and their animal furs, the passengers were warm and comfortable. The cold air plucked at the small areas of exposed skin on their faces.

The dogs sped across the flat ice. The only noise was the gentle hiss of the runners as they etched lines on the ice.

As they approached the end of the frozen lake, Everton notice a dark patch on the ice to his left, about four hundred metres from land and four hundred metres from their route.

As they reached the end of the lake, they passed onto gently rising land, with pine forest on either side. A gap ran up the valley between the trees, clearly where a stream ran after the winter thaw. Oskár called his dogs to a halt at the edge of the blue ice of the lake, and the three dog teams following also halted. They had been travelling for about an hour.

"We will now let you move a bit and have a warm drink," said Vulle to his clients.

Ánne, Oskár, and Sárá passed small cups of hot coffee and tea to the travellers from thermos flasks. Henry, Beth, Jean, and Everton stood, stretched, and walked in small circles, getting their joints and circulation moving.

"This is fabulous and gigantic scenery," said Jean to Sárá. "How far have we come?"

"Ten kilometres from the camp," said Sárá in her perfect English, with a slight American accent.

Everton stared at the dark patch on the ice about four hundred metres from the shoreline. "What's up with the ice over there?"

"There is an area of thin ice," said Vulle. "This is quite a new thing. We only noticed it this winter. Elsewhere the ice is several feet thick. But just there, the ice seems to be thinner. Sometimes it melts altogether. It might be a small area of geothermal hot water. But in Norway we normally only have geothermal springs on the coast. Perhaps it is due to climate change. But the ice is affected only in that very small area. It is a bit of a mystery."

"Perhaps we are seeing the birth of a new volcano," said Sárá. "We have volcanos in Norway too."

"We steer clear of that patch. You are quite safe with us on the thick ice," said Vulle.

Ahead of them, a valley led uphill, cutting between two mountains, rising from the flat ice plain they had been crossing.

Sárá pointed up the valley. "We will be climbing a little now, up this valley. Another two or three hours and we should reach our next camp if the weather remains clear. We have cabins and some tents there, called lavvu. You might want to try one of the lavvu. Very warm and comfortable. Lavvu are better than cabins, I think. If you want to become a true Sami lady, you should try a lavvu, Jean."

"Do the lavvu have en suite bathrooms and flushing toilets?" said Jean.

Sárá laughed. "Not at present. Perhaps we should add these for our English guests," she said.

Vulle and Oskár walked among the dogs, checking their harnesses and rubbing their heads. The dogs yapped and whined in an excited response, pleased to have attention, and looked at the humans as if to say, "What on earth are we waiting for? Why would anyone stop running if they had a choice?"

The countryside was silent apart from the dogs. As they were preparing to depart, in the distance, they heard the long and mournful howl of a wolf. Vulle looked up and smiled. They all stopped and listened. A few seconds later there was an answering howl from another wolf. The howls seemed to come from the valley ahead of them and echo down the valley. The dogs all turned to face up the valley and replied with a chorus of barks. The four travellers looked at Vulle, half smiling and half doubtful.

"Long way away," said Vulle. "In the mountains. They know we are here. They probably heard us crossing the lake, and they are staying clear of us. Warning each other that the humans are coming. To them, humans are hunters. We are a threat, not a meal."

Jean, Everton, and Beth shared their admiration of the grand scale of the mountain scenery illuminated by their torches. The darkness seemed to increase the scale of the landscape. Henry stood with them, also looking up at the mountains, but he was silent and frowning.

"Are you OK, honey?" said Beth.

"Mm-hm," said Henry.

Beth rubbed Henry's back and gave his arm a squeeze.

"Anyone who needs a toilet break can go now if you really have to," said Vulle.

The travellers looked around at the hard ice and freezing snow. Unzipping and unfastening multiple layers of warm clothes and exposing their warm, pink skin to the arctic air was sufficient to convince them all that they could cope for another leg of the journey.

"Anyone who wants to have a turn driving the sled can do this now. We will be climbing the valley ahead. Our speed will be a little less. The dogs are very kind and will look after you.

They will stop if you fall off," said Vulle with a smile. His family turned to the tourists, smiling, and waited for them to respond.

"It's a yes from me," said Jean.

"Me too," said Everton.

Beth looked at Henry. "I'll give it a try, I think, Henry," she said.

Henry blew air out and rubbed his chin. "Perhaps later for me. I'll stick to the first-class seat," he said.

Oskár, Sárá, and Vulle gave Jean, Everton, and Beth a short refresher on the dog calls, how to start the sled, how to use the claw brake to stop the sled, and commands for left and right. Ánne helped cover Henry with his fur blanket, and he settled into his sled without a murmur.

As they stood on their sleds, the dogs turned their heads, yelping in anticipation again. Oskár gave the cry to start, and his dogs shot into snow towards the valley rising ahead. The three following dog teams immediately followed the lead team.

Within a couple of hundred metres, Everton leaned the wrong way when the track curved slightly, and his sled toppled onto its side. He sprawled in the snow and rolled away from the sled. Vulle expertly stood and walked around the sled as it toppled over, lifted the sled upright, and stepped on the claw brake while shouting to the dogs. The dogs came to a halt and looked back at the driver lying on his stomach in the snow. Their eyes seemed to say, "We've got one of those daft English drivers this time."

Everton was lying on his side. The looks on the faces of the dogs reminded him of his mother when he had made a particularly stupid mistake. A mixture of understanding and exasperation. Vulle helped Everton to stand in the deep snow, and the dogs immediately started yelping to resume their journey. The three other sleds were now half a kilometre ahead. Despite Everton's inexperience, once they resumed their journey, his dogs quickly caught the rest of the sleds.

The ground was rising. They entered the pine forest that encircled the lake as they left the frozen lake behind. The forest absorbed most of the sound as they passed. For the lower part of their climb, they followed a forest track. As the slope increased, the speed of the dogs slowed slightly. Ahead they could see the forest ending and then, beyond this, the mountain pass between two peaks. The trees on either side of them at the lower reaches of the valley were densely packed. The darkness in the trees was even darker than the sky above them.

As they sped upwards, Everton's head torch caught two red dots shining out from one tall pine tree on his left side. Everton concentrated his torch on the dots, and his eyes managed to discern the silhouette of a huge owl with prominent ear tufts staring back. As he watched, as if it disapproved of the human intrusion into its domain, the owl let out a deep and resonant ooh-hu, spread its wings, and glided effortlessly across their track, above their heads, disappearing over the tops of tall pine trees to their right. It was as if the owl wanted a closer look, to see if these creatures were edible.

The lights of several more torches from Jean, Beth, and Vulle also followed the giant owl as it soared above them. Henry's torch had been switched off, and Henry seemed to be ignoring his surroundings. His neck and face protector covered most of his face, and his hood was drawn down over his eyes.

The four sleds advanced steadily up the valley, and the forest gradually thinned out. Eventually they emerged into smooth snow. Head torches were switched off one by one until only Oskár's head torch picked out their trail on the lead sled. Although it was dark, a crescent moon gave a faint light, and the Milky Way was emblazoned across the sky. As their eyes adapted to the darkness, Jean and Everton could see features of the mountains quite clearly. The dogs had no difficulty and advanced up the track, shouting occasional yelps of delight to one another.

As they reached the pass at the top of the valley, Oskár brought his sled to a halt, and the following sleds also stopped. They had now been sledding for just over three hours. From the mountain pass, ahead they could see that the track descended for several kilometres towards flatter land to the east, with smaller rolling hills and patches of forest rather than mountains. The entire landscape was covered in thick snow. It was midafternoon and still as dark as midnight.

"We take another short break here," said Vulle to the tourists, handing out cups of warm coffee again.

Henry was still sitting on his sled without speaking.

"Did you see that eagle owl? It flew over our heads. Fabulous," said Everton to Jean.

"This we call an *orn ugle* in Norwegian," said Vulle. "You are interested in birds, Everton?"

"Oh yes, he is," said Jean. "He is always interested in birds. He can spot a pregnant female chaffinch from two hundred metres. Don't get him started talking about birds."

"You won't see many birds at this time of year because of the permanent darkness. But the eagle owls hunt at night, so darkness helps them," said Vulle.

Vulle bent over Henry and touched his shoulder. "Would you like a drink, Henry?" said Vulle.

Henry's head came up suddenly, as if he had been asleep. "Oh. Drink. Yes, please. Thanks, Vulle," said Henry. He climbed off his sled and tried to stand. He struggled, and Vulle helped him rise to a standing position.

"How are you feeling?" asked Vulle, looking closely at Henry's face.

"Not too good at the moment," said Henry. "I feel stiff and sore all over. Time for a toilet break for me. That should sort things out."

Henry moved fifty metres from the group of sleds, faced away from the group, and started to unzip his outer clothes. Everton and Vulle both joined him, and they formed a group of men doing the necessary. All three men eventually uncovered enough to allow them to relieve themselves on the snow. As they stood in silence, listening to the gentle patter on the fresh snow, Everton noticed something slightly different about the colour of the traces they left in the snow. Henry's marks seemed darker. As he looked at the traces, from lower down the valley they had just travelled, another wolf called, mournful and threatening. Almost immediately, a second wolf called, this time a little closer and louder. The sled dogs answered the wolves, barking and facing back towards the valley behind them.

"We shouldn't stay here too long. The wolves don't normally take much interest in us. For some reason, they are more curious than usual. Perhaps they have a taste for English and American meat?" said Vulle with a broad grin.

Once they were finished, the three men zipped and fastened their multiple layers of warm clothing. Henry turned and started walking back to the sleds, slightly unsteady in the deep snow.

Both Vulle and Everton paused, allowing Henry to walk ahead, and switched on their head torches. They had both noticed the same thing about the colour of the marks in the snow. They pointed their torches at the ground in front of them. The traces left in the snow by Henry were very different to the pale yellow and gold of those from Everton and Vulle. Everton and Vulle looked at each other steadily for a few seconds. The marks left by Henry in the snow were clearly dark red or even black in places.

CHAPTER 4

Blood

As he reached his sled, Henry sat down heavily, breathing deeply, and groaned. He had walked only fifty metres, but he was breathless and panting.

Vulle caught up with him, leaned over, and placed a hand on Henry's back. "How are you feeling?" said Vulle.

"Not good. I feel nauseous," said Henry, swallowing hard.

Henry leaned forwards suddenly and vomited onto the snow. Everyone turned and looked at the snow. Several head torches shone on the patch next to Henry's sled. There was no doubt—the stain on the snow was bright red.

Henry groaned again.

Beth ran to Henry's side and put her arms around his shoulders. "Henry, honey. I think we had better head back home. I don't think you are up to this trip at present," said Beth, turning to Vulle. "Can we go back? Henry is not well enough to go on."

There was a pause, during which the Sami family members looked at one another.

"One moment please, Beth. We will think carefully how to help Henry," said Vulle. He beckoned to his family.

Ánne, Oskár, and Sárá walked to Vulle, and they talked for several minutes in Sami. The two adults listened carefully to their children. Sárá pointed back down the valley and then forwards towards the plain to the east as she spoke. Vulle and Ánne did most of the listening. There was a pause, during which Sárá looked up to the sky. At that moment, the northern lights flickered into life again. Veils of bright blue, yellow, pink, and green rippled and danced across the sky. They all looked up except for Henry, and despite the illness of one of their group, the lights were spellbinding.

Sárá was standing close to Jean.

"*Guovssahas*," said Sárá. She turned to Jean. "In Sami, this means 'the lights you can hear.' Can you hear the lights?"

"I think I can hear a faint crackling, or hissing," said Jean. "Is that what you mean?"

"Ja. Yes. I can hear it too. Not many people can hear this. It is unusual, especially for people from the south. This might be because you are a healer. You have the healing ability, and this gives you some stronger powers," said Sárá directly to Jean.

Jean raised her eyebrows, looked at Everton, and then looked back at Sárá and replied, "Yes, I suppose you could say that I am a healer of sorts. But I'm not sure that is linked to my hearing."

"I think Henry has a problem with his kidneys," said Vulle. "We saw signs of this over there." Vulle pointed to where the three men had taken a call of nature. "And now it seems he has a problem with his stomach also. Firstly, he needs to rest when we can get him somewhere warm. Then if he doesn't improve, we need to call for medical help."

A long, high-pitched howl echoed down from the mountain to the north. The dogs stood and answered this with yapping and barking.

Sárá pointed up the mountain, looked at her parents, then turned to the tourists. "This was a fox. This is a good sign, but also a warning," she said.

Vulle and his family seemed to reach a decision. Vulle turned to the tourists. "I think we must go on first. We are close to a wilderness cabin ahead. There we can get warm again. We can be there in less than an hour. We can stay there for a few hours and let Henry recover. We think that Henry will get better there quite quickly. We can go on to Camp Trollfjell tomorrow."

"I'm not sure, Vulle," said Beth, tears rolling down her cheeks and freezing in place instantly. "How do you know that Henry will be better there? Should we not get him to a hospital as soon as possible? All this blood. He is clearly bleeding from somewhere."

"If we turn back, it will be many hours before we can get back to Camp Arktis. Also, we do not have much left to drink, and we will be travelling for several hours. We don't think this is the best choice. Henry will be colder for longer if we turn back," said Vulle.

Little Sárá walked to Beth and put her arms around her, at least as far around as she could reach. Sárá said something in Sami, and then, "Henry will be better soon. We need to warm him up first, and then he will feel better. You can trust us. We know this country. We have seen this sort of thing often."

Jean, Everton, and Beth looked at Sárá. It was odd that a small girl of less than ten years should take the lead and be so confident in this serious situation. But they all felt reassured by Sárá. In an unusual way, her certainty was infectious.

Vulle and Ánne watched Beth and Sárá carefully and waited for their decision.

"Why do you think that Henry will get better, honey? How do you know this? You are so young. When did you learn about this?" said Beth.

"Not everything is learned. Some things we know because we feel them. I have a feeling about Henry and about his illness. This time I feel that it is better to go east and warm Henry as soon as possible. My people also believe that there are signs from nature that help us to make decisions. Some of the signs we have been seeing since we left Camp Arktis tell us to go forwards to the wilderness cabin first. We need to take each step at a time, I think you say in English," said Sárá.

"We will do this only if you agree, Beth," said Vulle. "If you insist, we will take Henry back to Camp Arktis, even though this is a long journey for him at present. We will respect your decision."

There was a long pause while Beth looked around at each of her companions. Henry remained silent. At length, Beth breathed in deeply. "OK. OK. Whatever you think is best, honey," said Beth, and she patted Sárá on her head, smiled at Vulle, and nodded.

Vulle nodded back, spoke a few words of Sami to his family, and moved to his sled at the back of the group to prepare the dogs. As he walked towards the sled, another wolf bayed from the valley behind them. It was a long, mournful, lonely call. It was slightly louder, so much nearer than previous calls.

Sárá said something to her family in Sami and pointed her gloved hand back down the valley. Her body language suggested she might be saying, "You see? I told you so."

The Issákson family took over the sled driving and mounted the footboards. Henry was already back on his sled, and Ánne tucked his reindeer-hide blanket tightly around him. He nodded in appreciation but said nothing. Jean, Everton, and Beth settled themselves on their sleds and wrapped their hide blankets closely around their legs. Everyone pulled up their mouth and nose coverings against the fierce cold.

"Mush," shouted Oskár, who was on the lead sled again. His dogs leaped into a run, yelping with delight. The four sleds slid down the slope towards the snowy plain below.

While they had been paused, clouds had blown overhead. As the sleds advanced through the crisp snow, it started snowing again. Within minutes, visibility had reduced to less than ten metres. From each sled, only the sled in front or behind could be seen. The stars and sky disappeared in the haze of snowflakes.

The dogs appeared unaffected by the snow and simply ran on without pause. There were still occasional barks from the lead dogs on each team, but the sound was muffled by the snow.

Everton was in the hindmost sled, with Vulle driving. He became aware of what seemed like occasional barks from behind him. Since there was no sled and no dogs following his sled, this did not seem quite right. Everton turned to look behind. At first, he could see nothing but snow. As he peered into the darkness with his head torch on, he caught sight of an occasional dark shape. As they moved forwards, he became aware of more dark shadows just at the limit of his vision. Some of these shadows appeared stationary, and the sled moved rapidly past. Some shadows seemed to be moving, keeping up with the sled. Suddenly a tall shape loomed out of the darkness and resolved into the white bark of a large birch tree. The sled slid soundlessly past the tree.

Of course, thought Everton, *we are descending into forest again. But trees don't bark. What is that noise behind us?*

As they travelled on, more trees slid past them on either side. Everton still thought he could hear an occasional bark from behind them. Just a short sound. Similar to the sled dogs, but a little deeper.

"Can you hear that?" said Everton to Vulle.

"What are you hearing?" said Vulle.

"I think I can hear something barking following us. Perhaps a fox? Or a wolf?"

Vulle turned and looked back, standing on the footboards at the back of the sled.

"The forest and the snow can make fools of us sometimes," said Vulle, without committing himself. "I hear something, but it is not clear."

Without warning, a blurred shadow darted out of the falling snow to the right of the sled, a few metres ahead of Everton, and lunged towards the lead dog. It was a blur to Everton, just on the edge of his field of vision, partially concealed by the falling snow. There was a deep growl from somewhere, but the direction was hard to identify. It might have been one of the sled dogs, but it seemed all around the sled. Then the lead dog on Everton's sled gave a loud bark, and the pace of the sled seemed to increase slightly.

Everton turned to look at Vulle. Vulle was frowning and concentrating his attention to the right of their sled. It was clear that Vulle was aware of the shadowy figure that seemed to have jumped at their lead dog for a fraction of a second. Vulle shouted to the dogs to speed up even more. They needed no encouragement, and the sled skimmed along the snow even faster. Vulle leaned down and slid his rifle case from behind Everton, where it had been stashed. He looped it over his shoulder by the strap.

He then looked down where Everton sat, smiled, and gave a thumbs-up sign without saying anything.

Shadowy trees were appearing more frequently as they descended the hill. Gradually it became clear to Everton that they were travelling along a well-established track that ran through the birch forest. Everton watched carefully either side of the sled. Three or four times, his head torch picked up one or two red points of light for a brief moment. Some of these were to his left, but others were to the right. Whatever they were, these animals were keeping up with the sled or even travelling faster than the sled. Everton could just see the sled in front, on which Henry and Ánne were travelling, through the blizzard of snow.

The ground levelled out. They had clearly reached the plain. The sleds did not slow. The dogs ran on tirelessly. Pine trees were densely packed on either side of the track they followed.

Everton turned to face Vulle. "Do you see the eyes reflecting our torch light on either side of the track?" said Everton.

"Yes. It has been following us since the mountain pass," said Vulle.

"Wolves, do you think?"

"One wolf."

"Not a pack then?"

"No. Just one wolf," said Vulle.

"I thought they travelled in packs."

"This is not a normal wolf. It may not be following us. It may be guiding us."

"Really? Where does it want us to go?" said Everton.

"I cannot be sure. It certainly does not want us to turn back. I think it has been following us since Camp Arktis. Or perhaps just following one of us," said Vulle.

"Is this normal? Does this happen very often?"

"Not often. The Sami believe that there is a wolf spirit, Suologievra. The Norse people also believe that there are wolf spirits who act as the eyes and ears of the gods. Perhaps it is one of these spirits that is following us," said Vulle, and he smiled down at Everton.

"Well, that's an interesting interpretation. Could it not just be a lone wolf following us hoping to pick up some food?" said Everton.

"That is possible. You should ask Sárá about it. She has read many books about this, and she is very knowing about these matters," said Vulle.

They had been travelling for less than an hour since their last stop when the trees thinned out and they emerged into a small clearing. The shape of a wooden cabin appeared out of the blizzard. Oskár brought his dog team to a halt, and the three following sleds pulled up alongside the cabin.

As the sleds stopped, a large raven landed on a tall birch tree at the edge of the clearing. He watched the travellers through the snow blizzard as they dismounted their sleds. From the sleds, Sárá turned and looked up at the raven. Jean watched Sárá as she stared up. The raven dipped its head several times and let out a loud gurgling croak that could be heard through the falling snow.

"That is a curious raven," said Jean, as she stood up from the sled.

"Yes. He is very interested in us," said Sárá. "He is probably looking after us. He sees that we have reached shelter, so he is happy. He is a friend and wants us to be safe."

"I see," said Jean, with a slight frown, staring at the tree on which the raven was perched.

Sárá started to unharness her dogs.

"Why do you think the raven was interested in us?" said Jean, as she tried to help with one of the dog's harnesses.

Sárá stood up and paused before answering, as if she were thinking of the best way to explain it to Jean. "The Sami believe that many spirits can take the form of animals or humans. Sometimes these spirits take an interest in us. We can't tell why this is often, at least until much later, and then we understand what is happening. I watch the animals and try to understand if their behaviour is unusual or unlike our wild animals."

"So you think this raven is a spirit disguised as a raven?" said Jean.

"I can't be sure. But it is not behaving quite like a normal wild raven. It is too familiar with us and too interested in us. Also, it is alone, when most ravens live in groups. And it has been following us on and off for many kilometres of our journey. It stopped when we stopped in order to get a good look at us. I get the feeling it is curious about us. Don't you get that feeling from it?"

Jean looked steadily at the raven. It looked straight back at her with one bright and shiny eye. She almost thought she detected it nodding gently at her. It also seemed very large. Larger than any raven she had ever seen, in fact.

"It does seem bright and alert. I wasn't aware it was following us. You must have eyes like an…like an eagle, to see details of animals in this dark and in the blizzard."

"It is all about practice. This is my country. I have lived here all my life. I am used to looking for these things. If you lived with us for ten years, you would start seeing what I see. You can stay with us and become like the Sami if you want to, you know. Mr. Everton could work for the police department in Norway."

"That is a very generous offer, Sárá. Thank you. But I have a life and a job in England. And so does my husband. It would be nice to live in your country, but we would have to give up everything we have built in England."

"That's all right, Jean. I understand," said Sárá. "I think you will take a little piece of Norway back to England with you when you fly home."

Sárá busied herself unharnessing the dogs while Jean continued to watch the raven. It stared back at her without moving.

"It almost seems as if it is listening to and understanding us," said Jean.

Just as Jean finished speaking, the raven raised its beak, cried out with several repeated gurgling sounds, and then took off and flew away into the blizzard.

"Or perhaps laughing at us," said Jean.

CHAPTER 5

Wilderness Cabin

AFTER THE FOUR SLEDS stopped next to the cabin, the dogs were silent for several seconds. As they were released from their harnesses, one by one, the silence was punctuated by their loud and rapid barking. They seemed to know they had arrived at their destination for the night. They appeared to be delighted with their performance, which was admittedly marvellous, and they were clearly expecting food and a rest, which was also well deserved.

Snow continued to fall thickly, but Vulle's family were calm and efficient. They quickly cleared snow from the cabin door and ushered the tourists inside. Jean and Beth entered the cabin. Inside, it was surprisingly spacious. A small wood-burning stove sat in one corner, with some firewood ready stacked next to it. There were three simple wooden bunk bed frames along one wall, sufficient for six of them. The cabin even had a wooden table and four chairs. Everything seemed to be made from wood except the glass in the windows and the cast-iron stove.

Henry was suffering and unable to speak. He was helped to a bunk bed by Vulle and Everton, where he lay on a sleeping bag and closed his eyes.

Vulle went out to settle and feed the dogs while Ánne and Sárá lit a fire in the stove and lit candles for light. Oskár unpacked the sleds and brought their travelling sacks into the cabin. They worked with quiet efficiency, only occasionally speaking in Sami to one another. Within half an hour, they had water boiling on the stove. Ánne took out some dried food from the supplies they had stowed on one of the sleds. Frozen fish, dried vegetables, and berries went into a pot and magically turned into a hot fish soup in no time. She also thawed some frozen flatbread she had brought, on the stove.

Jean and Everton sat at the table, feeling rather useless.

"Did you see any animals in the forest on the last stretch leading to the cabin?" said Everton to Jean.

"I don't think so. Visibility was very limited due to the snow. They would have had to come very close for me to see them. What sort of animals do you mean?" said Jean.

"I thought I might have seen an animal, perhaps a wolf, running alongside our sled. I think it was growling at our dogs, but I never really got a good look at it. I kept seeing shadows around the sled, on both sides, but the shadowy trees also confused me as we passed them. Vulle told me about some legends that the Sami have, about wolf spirits, or wolf men. It was quite spooky. I can see how easy it is to believe in these supernatural ghosties and ghoulies out here in blizzard conditions," said Everton.

"I don't think I saw any animals during the blizzard. But I wasn't really looking, and visibility was down to only about ten paces. There could have been a whole pack of wolves running with us, and I wouldn't have seen them. The dogs didn't seem worried. They seemed to be running for joy the whole way," said Jean.

Once the hot soup was ready, Sárá sat Henry up on his bed and fed him a bowl of soup slowly, with small pieces of the flatbread. Henry ate what he could, with help, but without speaking, and then he lay back and immediately fell asleep.

Everton, Jean, and Beth sat at the table, where the children served them bowls of soup with flatbread. The stove was warming the cabin rapidly.

"This is absolutely delicious," said Jean to Ánne.

"Amazing. Thank you so much for this, Ánne," said Everton.

Ánne smiled and nodded in appreciation as her family also ate the soup.

By the time the soup was finished, the cabin had warmed significantly. They were all able to take their full body suits and outer coats off and stretch their legs.

Vulle and Oskár went out to gather some more of the chopped firewood, which was stacked against one wall of the cabin.

Bathroom facilities were rudimentary and of the natural outdoor type. The snow had stopped again, and the sky was dark and clear overhead, but the temperature outside had plummeted even further. They took it in turns to dart into the forest and do what nature demanded, as quickly as possible. While anyone was outside, Vulle stood outside the cabin door keeping a watch, with his rifle in hand.

Once they were all back inside the cabin, Beth moved one of the chairs next to Henry's bed and sat holding his hand.

Jean and Everton sat at the table with Vulle. Oskár lay on a bunk bed.

Ánne and Sárá each sat on Henry's bunk bed.

Without any explanation or fuss, Sárá felt Henry's forehead, gently pulled one of his lower eyelids down to look at the white of his eye, then felt the pulse at his wrist, and looked closely at both of his hands. There was a slight blue colouring of his fingers, especially at the bases of his nails. Throughout this novel examination by a nine-year-old girl, Henry remained fast asleep, or at least unresponsive. Sárá turned to her mother and said something softly in Sami. Ánne nodded to her daughter.

Jean and Everton looked at each other with raised eyebrows, seeing this unusual young girl acting like the cabin doctor.

"Has Henry ever suffered anything like this before?" Sárá said to Beth.

"Never been like this before," said Beth, shaking her head. "Henry is very strong and healthy normally. He could lose twenty pounds, but then so could we both. I would have thought his extra body insulation would help him in these temperatures. But he takes no medication. Hasn't seen a doctor for years."

"Has Henry ever been to cold places like Norway before?" said Sárá.

"We live in Florida, honey. At this time of year in Florida, we can swim in the sea, which is eighty degrees Fahrenheit. We have never even been to the northern United States before this trip. This is our first trip outside the US and our first trip to anywhere cold. We got passports for the first time for our journey here," said Beth.

Sárá spoke to Ánne and Vulle in Sami. Sárá seemed to be trying to persuade her parents about something.

"I think we can move tomorrow to Camp Trollfjell," said Vulle. "There we have access to some first-aid facilities. We can contact the emergency services in Tromsø if Henry doesn't improve. If necessary, we can ask for a medical helicopter for him."

"How long will it take to get to Camp Trollfjell?" said Beth.

"If the snow has stopped, we should be there within two hours. The rest of your group, the ones who are using snowmobiles, will already be there waiting for us," said Vulle.

Sárá and Ánne cleared and cleaned their bowls and cutlery from the meal using melted snow water. Vulle and Oskár then went out to check on the dogs. Everton took the opportunity to put his layers back on and stretch his legs, and then he followed the two Sami outside.

Outside, the snow had stopped falling, and the temperature was painfully low. The still air was very cold on Everton's face. Condensation from their breath, on their eyelashes, turned to ice instantly. The sky was clear above the forest clearing, and the crescent moon cast a pale blue light on the snowy landscape. The moonlight was sufficient that no head torches were needed for reasonable vision. As the cold air hit Everton's face, water vapor in his breath froze as he breathed out. Their sleds were now just white mounds in the snow. The dogs had eaten and were curled up in the snow, resting or sleeping, with snow piled on their backs and heads. Some of the dogs were completely covered in snow. As Vulle and Oskár walked around the pack ruffling their heads, one of the lead dogs stood and shook the snow off his fur. The dog was slightly larger than most of the others. His fur was black, with pale yellow around his face and two yellow dots above his eyes. The yellow dots made it look as if he had an extra set of eyes. His real eyes were bright blue in the moonlight. He nuzzled against Vulle's leg and then turned to face west, back along the track they had followed to get to the cabin.

"This is Čammo. He is one of my best dogs. He is a very good friend. He knows what I think before I do," said Vulle, rubbing the dog's head.

Čammo stood perfectly still, facing west, and growled. It was a deep and sinister sound. Not friendly.

Vulle looked in the same direction as the dog for a few seconds and then up at the sky. The Milky Way was clear in a spectacular stripe across the sky.

Everton looked in the same direction as the dog and Vulle.

Oskár pointed along the track they had used and said something to Vulle in Sami. Vulle replied, and Oskár turned to Everton.

"I think Čammo can see something that is not clear to us," said Oskár.

Very faint, and very distant, there was a solitary wolf cry. Again Čammo growled, low and deep, still standing stock still and facing west. The hair on his back stood up.

"I can tell you a good story," said Oskár, with a broad grin on his face. "We have a legend in the Sami people about the wolf spirit. His name is Suologievra. Sami believe that he can move between the worlds. Čammo might have seen, or sensed, Suologievra. Sami believe that dogs like Čammo, with the spots above his eyes, have an extra pair of magical eyes. If you believe these legends, it is possible that Suologievra has been following us for a few hours, or even days. He might be protecting us. Or perhaps pushing us. Guiding us. Or perhaps just watching us. This might be a good sign, if you believe these things. Sárá knows more than me about these things. You should ask her to tell you more. She will talk you to sleep about it."

Everton looked along the forest track again. There was still no visible movement.

"Yes. Vulle mentioned the wolf-man while we were travelling. Perhaps Čammo can just smell wolves? Real wolves. Not spirit wolves," said Everton, smiling back at Oskár.

There was a pause.

"Perhaps," said Oskár, and he smiled at Everton.

Everton looked up at the stars, and as he did so, he thought he detected movement in his peripheral vision, just out of visual range, in the direction Čammo was facing, along the forest track. Everton peered intently along the track again but could not see anything.

Čammo licked his lips, sat down, and curled up, resting his head on his front paws. Suddenly he seemed bored.

Vulle gave the dog one more stroke and then turned back to the cabin door, followed by Oskár and Everton.

"If Henry is well enough, I am sure we will be able to move to Camp Trollfjell tomorrow. Since it is not much more than two hours from here, Henry should not have a problem making it. We have some cabins; some lavvu, which are tents; a generator; and some basic medical equipment there. The roads are not clear at present, but we have plenty of stores there. If Henry is not well enough to move, we can last there as long as we need to. It is even possible to request a medical helicopter in an emergency," said Vulle to Everton.

"Thank you, Vulle. I am very grateful for your help. It's just unfortunate that Henry became ill when we were out in the countryside. We understand. We are still enjoying the northern lights and the Norwegian countryside. In a way, this detour has given us an even more authentic Sami experience. This is what we really came for, I suppose—without the illness for Henry, of course," said Everton.

They stamped the snow off their boots at the cabin door. Jean, Beth, and Sárá were lying on bunks. Henry still appeared to be sleeping. He had eaten only a very small amount, but nobody wanted to disturb him. Ánne was preparing sleeping bags and furs for her and Vulle to sleep on the floor.

Sárá sat up as the men entered the cabin. Vulle spoke to Sárá in Sami and pointed to Everton. Sárá replied in Sami and turned to Everton.

"My father tells me that you saw the wolf spirit, Suologievra, outside. You are very lucky if he has shown himself to you. He was following us from the moment we left Camp Arktis. This is not a bad thing. As long as we are respectful, this is good," said Sárá.

Vulle and Ánne said nothing. They just watched their small daughter telling the strangers about their traditional beliefs.

"Really. I was not sure what I saw out there. Your beliefs are certainly very new to me. Tell us more about this wolf spirit," said Everton, sitting at the table.

The cabin was warm, and the lights of the candles sent flickering shadows dancing over the walls.

"The name Suologievra means 'powerful and strong of the island,'" said Sárá. "You see, the world of men is considered to be like an island. The Sami believe that Suologievra travels between the lower, middle, and upper worlds. These are what the Christians might think of as heaven, hell, and earth. You can see that different people often share similar legends. The wolf spirit is considered a friend of the noaidi, who are our shaman, or priests. The noaidi are our healers too, but they also forecast the weather and rescue lost souls. For Sami people, if Suologievra was following and guiding us, this is a good thing, because he is protecting us," said Sárá.

Ánne, Oskár, and Vulle sat back and watched as little Sárá conducted her master class in Sami folklore.

"Do you think that the dogs knew this Suologievra was following us?" said Jean.

"Oh yes. The dogs know much more than we do. They can see, hear, and smell much more than we can. Suologievra will have talked to the dogs while we were travelling," said Sárá.

"I think I remember some similar legends in the folklore of the Norse people. They also talk about wolf spirits," said Jean.

"You're right, Jean," said Sárá. "The Norse people have legends of their god Odin. This is the one with only one eye, you will remember. The father god. They say that Odin has two ravens, Huginn and Muninn, and two wolves, Geri and Freki, who wander the world. Midgard is their name for our world. They believe that the ravens and wolves act as Odin's eyes and ears around our world. Some people think Odin is the raven god because of his two speaking ravens. Now, the names are interesting. Odin is also known as Woden. Your English day Wednesday comes from the word *Woden*. You English are closely descended from the Norse people, who conquered England many times. Many Norse people moved from the north to England to live more than a thousand years ago. Some of our people liked your warmer climate. Also, the people of Normandy in France originally came from the Norse tribes. That is why they are called Normans. Your King William came from this tribe of Norsemen. We Sami came from farther east originally. We came from the Ural Mountains, which are now in Russia. Some Sami moved south too, as far as Scotland. The Sami were in the Urals before Russia existed. And we will probably still be there long after modern countries have gone," said Sárá.

"I suppose the wolves are important to the Sami because they can take your reindeer. And your reindeer are very important for your survival in the Arctic. You depend on the reindeer, and they depend on you. Wolves are a threat to both of you," said Everton.

In the candlelight, with the warm stove burning inside and the deep snow outside, Sárá was providing the tourists with a lesson in folklore that would be hard to forget. Henry appeared to be fast asleep. It seemed he was missing the chance of a lesson from a small Sami princess.

"This is true, Mr. Everton. We have another legend about wolves," said Sárá. "There is a saying that the wolf always finds his way. The tale is that a man called Stuorra-Jownna, or Jouni the Great, who was from a place called Utsjoki, wanted to change into a wolf. He knew some witches, who told him that, if he went around a curved tree counterclockwise several times, he would become a wolf. This might seem a little unlikely to us these days, but in ancient times, the rules of the world were different. Anyway, Jouni found a curved tree, which is not very difficult if you look hard, walked around it as instructed, and changed into a wolf. He was able to move around in the shape of a wolf for several weeks at a time before he had to return to his human shape to avoid being stuck in the wolf shape. One day, he had been in the shape of a wolf for a long time, and he realised that his time as a wolf was ending on the same night. He was nine valleys distant from the tree where he had changed into a wolf. He had to get back to the same tree in time, or he would be doomed to stay as a wolf for the rest of his life. That night he ran through the nine valleys and reached the tree where he had changed into a wolf just in time. He ran around the tree clockwise and gradually changed back into a human. Since then, we have told this story. It is really about the wolf always getting to wherever it wants to."

"So, this legend is perhaps partly about the stamina of the wolf," said Jean. "The fact that wolves can run and run for miles and miles after their prey is one of their advantages against their prey. And of course, your dogs are descended from wolves, aren't they? The dogs can also run for hours and hours without a break. We saw that today. They have wonderful stamina. I wish I could run like that. They seem so joyful just running and running."

"And the wolves are also very intelligent," said Vulle. "The English killed off all their wolves centuries ago, I think. The wolf is also now an endangered species in Finland. There are only about two hundred left in Finland because men have hunted them. In Sami, the word for wolf is *gumpe*. You are right that the reason we fear the wolf is because they can kill our reindeer. Some people believe that wolves have a magic power to make humans sleep, which then allows them to take the reindeer. Sami sing songs called *joiks* while guarding our reindeer to deter wolves from attacking. But wolves are so clever that they soon learn the words of a joik if we sing the same joik too often. If they know the words of the joik, it will not scare them so much. So we have to sing different joiks, with new words, to keep the wolves away from our reindeer. Not many animals can remember the words of our songs. Ravens are also very clever animals. They can even learn to speak our words. I think you have ravens protecting your country. In your Tower of London.

"You see, our legends can tell us much about our own lives," said Sárá, nodding at Everton. "You tell us that you are having a long break from your work in England, Mr. Everton. I think you will learn something very useful from our rules of living in the

Arctic. Our beliefs and customs will be very useful to you. You will be able to use the knowledge you gain here to solve many crimes. You will be able to help Henry get better, and you will take what you learn back to England. I think this is true."

Sárá stared at Everton intently, as if she were looking through him.

Everton looked up at Vulle, who smiled, winked, and shrugged.

"Well, that is very interesting," said Everton. "You are full of surprises, young lady. I've learned a great deal about Sami folklore tonight. I hope you're right about it being useful when I get back to England. Now tell me, what do you want to do when you grow up?"

Sárá smiled and shook her head. "Don't you think I am a little young to be deciding that, Mr. Everton?" said Sárá. "I'm only nine years old. How could I possibly decide now? Did you know you wanted to be a policeman when you were nine years old? Don't you think I should just be a child and do childish things for a few more years?"

Everton laughed, then Jean laughed, then Sárá joined in, and soon everyone except Henry was laughing.

"You are right. Of course you must have your childhood first, Sárá. It was a daft question, but a very good answer. I had no idea I would work as a detective when I was nine. Although I did know I wanted to be a soldier when I was your age. I was in the army before I joined the police force," said Everton.

While Sárá entertained her guests, Vulle sat in the corner of the cabin listening. He held a small piece of wood in his rough hands. He was carving something with his knife.

Jean walked over to Vulle and sat next to him. "What are you carving, Vulle?" she said.

"I have nearly finished," said Vulle. "Let me just make this slight change. There. I think it is done. What do you think?"

Vulle held out the small object in his large, callused hand, and offered it to Jean. "Why, it is a wolf," said Jean. "A wolf running. It is beautiful, Vulle. You are a true craftsman. You should sell carvings. You could make a good living from carving."

"It is strange you say this, Jean," said Vulle, "because I do sell my carvings. When we get to Camp Trollfjell, you will see many more of them. But you keep that one. It is a gift to you and Mr. Everton, from me. It will protect you from harm." Vulle winked at Jean and smiled.

"That is so kind of you, Vulle," said Jean. "Thank you so much. We will treasure it."

Exhausted from their journey, warm and well fed in their cabin, the tourists and their Sami guides slept well overnight. Outside the cabin, a lone wolf kept watch from a safe distance, among the pine trees, hidden in the darkness of the permanent winter night. It might have been a lone male, looking for a new pack.

CHAPTER 6

Camp Trollfjell

THE SAMI FAMILY WERE already preparing breakfast when Everton and Jean woke. Somehow Ánne had rustled up a stew using dried reindeer meat and vegetables, which they ate with more flatbread, all heated on the wood-burning stove.

"This is absolutely delicious," said Jean.

"You sure know how to cook. I never tasted reindeer until this trip. We have reindeer in the States, but we call it caribou," said Beth.

Henry was feeling much better. He managed to sit up and eat a full helping of reindeer stew and drank plenty of water. He even managed to walk around the cabin a couple of times, stretching and stamping his feet.

"You are looking much better, Henry," said Sárá, as she packed her sleeping bag.

"Yep. I feel much better," said Henry. "Things are looking up. So sorry that I caused all this disruption. There is a silver lining to this slight problem I have. It has given me some good ideas for writing."

"What do you write about?" said Sárá.

"I write novels," said Henry. "I'm not very good, but I enjoy it. I write mostly about things I observe or experience, and I try to weave a story with some meaning around these events. So although it is not nice being ill, it might give me some context for my next book. What happens when you are on holiday in a hostile environment, and you suddenly become ill. How do people react to you. That sort of thing."

"That sounds very interesting," said Sárá. "I will definitely buy your next book. A first edition by Henry Gibson. I hope you will sign it for me."

"Better than that," said Henry. "I'll send you a signed copy. I'll even put you in it if you agree. I can change your name to protect your privacy, of course, if you prefer."

"I am flattered, Henry. Thank you for this. You can use my name if you want. And I suggest you might write about our Sami culture and our folklore if it is interesting enough. People in the heat of Florida might be fascinated by our life."

Henry paused and scratched his head. "You are right, Sárá. I think readers will find it very interesting. That's a great idea."

Vulle was outside, feeding the dogs. Henry decided to risk taking a look outside the cabin and stood looking into the surrounding forest. It was midmorning and still as dark as velvet midnight. The snow was deep on the ground and on the cabin roof, but there was no snow falling.

"How do you feel this morning?" said Vulle to Henry.

"Not too bad. In fact, you know what? I feel great. Back to normal. I think I am fine to travel for a couple of hours, or even longer. Hopefully I will remain well until we get to Camp Trollfjell. I'm sure looking forwards to meeting your reindeer," said Henry.

"Good, Henry. I hope we make good time today. You will be more comfortable at Camp Trollfjell. We will certainly see some reindeer there. A herd of our reindeer stays there over winter. They are a mixture of domestic and wild reindeer. It is a good time to experience reindeer. If you are up to it, we might even get in some hunting."

The Issáksons cleared away the sleeping kit, packed their luggage in hide bags, and stowed these on the sleds as efficiently and quietly as ever. They left the cabin as they had found it, perfect for the next visitors, with fresh firewood stacked next to the stove.

The Sami drove the sleds again for the trip to Camp Trollfjell. This time there were no signs of any wolves or foxes. They made good time through the forest, following wide tracks between the silver birch trees, which looked as if they had been cleared hundreds of years previously and used regularly. During the journey, they were all grateful for their multiple layers of warm clothes because the temperature remained very low. The dark sky remained clear of clouds. Stars were clearly visible in the middle of the day, in the stripe of sky visible above the forest track. Water vapor froze on their eyelashes and any other exposed hair.

Less than two hours after starting, the dogs sped out of the forest into a large clearing, at least a kilometre across. In the centre of the clearing sat a cluster of cabins, dimly lit by lights mounted above the doors, and several structures that appeared to be tents, similar in appearance to North American tipis. Snow lay deeply on all the cabins and tents. Reindeer were dotted around the edge of the clearing, and more could be seen and heard on the edge of the clearing and in the forest, grazing in a leisurely manner. As they grazed, the gentle clank of reindeer bells spread around the clearing. One or two of the reindeer looked up at the arrival of four sleds, dogs, and humans, then dropped their heads to carry on grazing in the snow. They were clearly very familiar with humans coming and going.

Snowmobiles were parked next to one of the larger buildings, which looked like a storage shed for the vehicles. Several people could be seen outside the cabins, moving around the clearing.

Oskár stood on his claw brake and brought his dogs to a halt outside one of the larger cabins. The following sleds stopped close to Oskár's.

This time Henry seemed to be affected by the journey even more. He did not respond when Vulle touched his shoulder on the sled. Vulle and Everton had to carry him into the cabin where he and Beth would be staying. They laid Henry on a bed, where he remained unresponsive.

Edo, the Sami driver, came to greet them. Vulle and Ánne spoke to Edo in Sami, explaining why they had been delayed overnight and telling him about Henry's recurrent illness. Edo updated Vulle on the snowmobile group, which had made good time to arrive the previous evening.

Vulle lit the wood burner in Henry's cabin. Sárá stayed with Henry and Beth while their cabin was warming.

Vulle showed Jean and Everton into their cabin. A generator was running, which provided light in each cabin. Vulle lit a wood-burning fireplace in each cabin. Their luggage and their backpacks were delivered to them. Very soon their cabins were warm enough for the tourists to take off their outer clothing.

After the tourists had all eaten lunch in the largest cabin, which served as a dining area, Vulle called a meeting to discuss their situation. Henry was the only person missing, still sleeping, or comatose, in his warm cabin, but Beth joined them.

"Welcome to Camp Trollfjell," said Vulle to the assembly of tourists. "Apologies for being late. We had to make a detour when Henry Gibson became ill on the journey here. This kept us away overnight. Edo has received some news from our Oslo office by satellite phone. There is now a temporary travel ban operating between countries in Europe, North America, and most of the Pacific countries. This has been put in place because of the two small outbreaks of illness in London and New York. We hope that the travel ban will be lifted swiftly, within a few days. Within Norway, there are also some limits to travel between large cities. We hope this will not affect us out here in the beautiful countryside. Also, it should not prevent us getting back to Tromsø. By the time we are back in Tromsø, in a couple of days, we hope that travel should be back to normal. We don't want anyone to worry. If there is any extension to your stay here in Norway, your travel insurance will certainly cover you."

The tourists looked at one another and started talking excitedly about the impact of this latest news.

"I am sorry to bother you, Vulle, but I really think that Henry needs medical attention very soon," said Beth. "I am scared that he is going to die. I think we should take him back to Tromsø, or even to Oslo, as soon as possible."

For a moment, nobody spoke. Then Vulle nodded. "I fully understand your concern, Beth. However, if we take Henry back to Tromsø, we would all need to make the journey together. To transport an ill man over such distance at this time of year, all of my family and Edo will need to come with us. This will mean that we cannot leave anyone here without expert Sami support. The climate is too dangerous. We could only do this if everyone agrees that this is the right course. Even then, I cannot guarantee that the authorities in Tromsø will even allow us to enter the city. We could attempt the journey, but I would not recommend it."

The three Dutch tourists were talking quietly among themselves in Dutch. They all seemed worried. Christiaan became slightly agitated, waved his hands at the other two, then rose to speak. "We are very much against going back to Tromsø, Vulle. We agree with you. We think it is very dangerous for Mr. Gibson to travel such a long way, in such a hostile environment. We would much prefer that Mr. Gibson is cared for here, to the best of your ability, and we would prefer to continue with our stay as originally planned. After all, we are not harming Mr. Gibson in any way by exploring your countryside."

Rolf, the elderly German, stood. "If my wife and I want to leave right now to return to Germany, will this be possible?" he said.

"Unfortunately, this is not possible," said Vulle. "Even if we travelled back to Tromsø today, and if we were allowed to enter Tromsø, you would not be allowed to travel across the Norwegian border."

Rolf and his wife frowned and looked at each other in disappointment. But Rolf sat without any audible protest.

Christiaan stood again to speak. "One more thing, Vulle. While we are at this camp, I hope that we will still be able to use the snowmobiles and enjoy the countryside? We don't need any help with this, other than the snowmobiles, so it will not take up your time," he said.

"Oh, ja. Yes indeed. You will still be able to enjoy our winter safari in Sami country," said Vulle. "We will be introducing you to our reindeer, and you can still enjoy our Sami hospitality. Nothing will change there. You must make the most of your time here."

"What is the nature of the American man's illness? With the outbreak in New York, we should be told about this," said Rolf, standing again.

Vulle paused. He looked across the dining hall at Ánne and Sárá, who were standing at the back.

"It seems that Mr. Gibson is particularly vulnerable to the cold. He has been badly affected each time we go outdoors. For now, we just want to keep him warm. I will be contacting the medical services in Tromsø this afternoon. I expect that they will send someone out to attend to him. I am sure there is no link with the illnesses in New York," said Vulle.

"With great respect, Mr. Vulle, you are not a doctor, I believe," said Rolf. "With such a serious illness in New York, should we not take some precautions to protect the rest of us?"

There was a low murmur from some of the other tourists.

"I can assure you that Henry is not a risk to the rest of us," said Vulle. "My family have been travelling with Henry for two days, as well as Mr. and Mrs. Everton. None of us have had any symptoms. Henry recovers fully once he warms up, which is not a sign of any contagious illness. Henry will remain in his cabin while he recovers his strength. I will keep you updated. Now thank you, everyone. We have some interesting encounters with reindeer planned for the afternoon. We will meet back here for our evening meal. I hope to have more information for you then from the medical services."

The tourists gradually dispersed. Rolf and his wife, Ulva, appeared to be having a heated debate about the situation in German. From their expressions, neither Rolf nor Ulva was very happy with the travel restrictions or the plans for Henry's illness.

The tourists dispersed to their cabins.

As Jean and Everton sat in their warm cabin, preparing for their afternoon with the reindeer, they talked over their situation.

"What do you think about the possibility that Henry has some serious infection, which he picked up in New York?" said Everton.

"Implausible. Really unlikely. I agree with Vulle," said Jean. "Firstly, he was only ill when he was out in the cold. As soon as we warmed him up, he recovered. Secondly, the rest of us were all perfectly well throughout the trip. If he had some sort of viral haemorrhagic fever, we would all be very ill, or even dead, by now, with bleeding, vomiting, and severe fevers. No, this looks like something unique to Henry, without any features of contagious infection. We need to guard against hysteria. Being in a remote location, with rumours from hysterical amateur journalists and a precautionary but alarming travel ban, is psychologically likely to produce irrational responses borne of fear. I think the elderly German couple were on the brink of suggesting that we expel Henry into the wilderness at the meeting."

"Yes. I agree. We should support Vulle in his attempts to keep the group calm," said Everton.

Jean and Everton spent the afternoon with Sárá and Oskár, who introduced them to several domesticated reindeer. Oskár carried bags of pellets and moss to where the herd were grazing. The reindeer started to approach him as he walked along, poking their noses towards his bags and sniffing. They clearly knew he had some goodies for them.

"These pellets help to keep them healthy," said Sárá. She pulled out a large knife and sliced open one of the bags on the ground. She held out a cupped hand with a pile of pellets on it.

A reindeer with huge antlers, at least ten times her weight, gently nuzzled her hand and ate the pellets from her hand.

"This reindeer is very friendly. You can stroke him if you like, but don't touch his antlers. If you do, he will shake you off. He might injure you by accident. He is very strong but very gentle. Stay calm, and he will not be afraid of you. If you show you are afraid, he will sense this, and he will be afraid," said Sárá, standing next to the reindeer, which was at least three feet taller than her.

Jean and Everton both also fed the huge reindeer with pellets. Once the other reindeer saw that the humans were calm and friendly, they started to nudge forwards to have a treat. One or two of them jostled for position, but they were all very gentle when they came near the humans. As they ate, the reindeer bells around some of their necks clanked and clonked reassuringly.

The sky to the south was a shade less dark than the rest of the sky, which was velvet black. This was a faint sign of the sun beneath the horizon in the midafternoon. The children were using their head torches for light among the reindeer.

"The eyes of this reindeer appear blue," said Everton, shining his torch at the nearest reindeer.

"Yes. The eyes of arctic reindeer change colour through the seasons from gold in summer to blue in winter," said Sárá. "This is an adaptation to extreme changes of light levels in their environment. In the arctic winter, their eyes collect more light. It helps the reindeer detect predators, like wolves."

"Professor Sárá lecture number one," said Oskár, in one of his rare comments about his sister.

Sárá ignored her big brother. She was clearly used to his teasing and felt he was not worthy of a response.

"And did you know that reindeer can see in the ultraviolet spectrum too?" said Sárá. "This also helps them to detect predators in winter. We cannot see it, but there is plenty of ultraviolet light around us here when there is little visible light. It is actually possible to get a tan, even in the darkness of the arctic winter, because of the ultraviolet light."

Jean and Everton took turns to sit on a low sleigh, to which the reindeer was harnessed, and took a short trip for several kilometres around a frozen lake close to the camp. Sárá led the reindeer holding a rope.

As she walked next to the reindeer pulling Jean on the sleigh, Sárá talked about the reindeer. "Over many thousands of years, we have convinced the reindeer that we want to look after them. They are much bigger than me, but some of them let me lead them without any objection. They know me, and they know that I will be kind to them. They are patient with me because I am patient with them. Even the wild reindeer will tolerate us more because they watch our reindeer and copy them."

Once Jean had dismounted the sleigh, Sárá announced their next exercise. "Now you must learn to lasso. This will be critically important when you become reindeer herders," she said.

Oskár had set a large set of reindeer antlers in a clear patch of snow. They stood ten metres away from the antlers, while Oskár took a long rope with a loop at one end and expertly threw it over the antlers. He easily snagged the antlers and pulled the noose tight two times out of three, narrowly missing his third throw. He then handed the lasso to Jean.

Jean also managed to snag the antlers twice out of three throws.

"Very good, Jean. You are a quick learner. You will make an excellent reindeer herder," said Oskár without a trace of a smile.

Everton tried five times with the lasso but missed each time.

"This is a shame, Mr. Everton. You should probably keep your job as a detective. You might be very hungry if you tried herding reindeer," said Oskár, this time with a hint of a smile.

Sárá then threw the lasso three times and snagged the antlers each time perfectly. "I must be lucky today," she said, beaming widely at Oskár.

As Sárá said this, they were treated to another light show in the sky. Ripples of golden green, blue, and violet moved above their heads, combining and separating. Even the two young Sami children were impressed. They all stood and stared for several minutes.

As the children were clearing up the ropes, a large raven flew down and landed on the antlers on the ground. The bird was as big as a medium-sized dog, with bright eyes and a fearsome-looking shiny black beak. The raven looked confidently at the two English tourists, then turned to the Sami children and emitted a series of low croaks.

"That is one huge bird," said Everton.

The raven turned its head towards Everton and emitted a gurgling croak, almost as if he were replying to Everton.

They all waited for the bird to fly away. Instead, it continued to perch on the antlers and turned back to face the two Sami children, as if waiting for them to do something.

Sárá walked slowly towards the raven and stopped within a couple of paces. She spoke a few words in Sami, facing directly towards the bird.

Oskár said something behind Sárá, but she held up her hand, and he stopped immediately. Her authority in matters of animal communication was obviously absolute to her brother.

For several minutes, Sárá spoke several words, then the raven croaked in apparent reply, then Sárá spoke again. It seemed like a conversation. This exchange continued for several minutes, back and forth between Sárá and the raven.

Jean and Everton watched in amazement.

Eventually, the raven bowed its head several times, wiped its beak on the antlers, spread its wings, and launched into the sky, flying away to the north, croaking loudly as it disappeared.

"That was amazing," said Jean to Sárá. "Do you know that raven? Is it a tame raven?"

"I might have met him before," said Sárá. "It is hard to tell with ravens. They all look alike."

Oskár said something in Sami to Sárá, and Sárá replied with a shrug.

"Animals come to Sárá often," said Oskár. "She has a way of knowing with them. They seem to like her more than most people. Probably because she doesn't talk them to death."

"What do you think the raven was saying?" said Jean.

Sárá looked away to the north, in the direction the raven had flown. "I can't say," she said after a long pause.

"You can't say, or you don't know?" said Jean.

"Don't be silly, Jean. Ravens can't talk to humans. You have been reading too many fairy stories," said Sárá, still staring after the departed raven.

Their fellow tourists chose various activities. The three young Dutch travellers each took snowmobiles and went out for a trip around the area on their own. They were confident of their navigation skills after the trip from Camp Arktis. The darkness in midafternoon changed only slightly. The sky changed from a velvet blackness to a dark grey, with a slight rosy tinge on the horizon to the south, in a tribute to the hidden sun below the horizon. The snowmobiles had excellent lights, so the winter darkness was not an obstacle.

After their reindeer exploits, Jean and Everton called on Beth and Henry. In their warm cabin, Beth was sitting next to Henry's bunk bed. Henry was lying on his side, facing away from Beth towards the wall, unresponsive.

"How is Henry getting on?" said Jean.

"Jean, I am so worried," said Beth. "Henry hasn't stirred since we arrived here. We have warmed him up. You can feel the heat in here from the wood burner. This time he has just remained as you see him. He looks like he is sleeping, but I can't wake him. He has had nothing to eat or drink for a whole day since the wilderness cabin. I have asked Vulle to get an air ambulance. He does not think this will be possible. I don't know what more I can do."

"I am sure Vulle is doing all he can. We can ask him for an update this evening," said Jean.

The tourists assembled in the early evening in the dining cabin for a meal. Only Henry and Beth were missing. The visitors were treated to reindeer blood pancakes, reindeer steak, and crusty bread, followed by cloudberry ice cream—an arctic feast.

"Fabulous ice cream. No problems with refrigeration around these parts," said Jean in a whisper to Everton as they finished their meal.

Once the meal was over, Vulle stood and addressed the group. "I have spoken to our office in Tromsø about the travel situation. No change so far to the travel restrictions. But no additional illnesses, apparently. It looks as if the medical authorities in England and America have contained the outbreak. I think that borders will be opened soon. This will all blow over, as they say in England."

Rolf stood again. "What news about our sick American?"

"He is still unwell. His wife is with him. I have contacted the medical authorities in Tromsø and Oslo. They are aware of his symptoms. They do not want to send any emergency services. Instead, they have told us we should remain at Camp Trollfjell until the travel ban is lifted," said Vulle.

"Did you ask the medical people to evacuate the American?" said Rolf.

"Yes," said Vulle.

"And?" said Rolf.

"As I said, they did not want to evacuate Henry at present," said Vulle.

"So they refused to take the sick American. They have imposed a local quarantine on us all in Camp Trollfjell. This is like the plague. They quarantined villages to allow the occupants to die. I think we need to focus on the best interests of the majority. The American should be expelled from the camp immediately. We are all at risk while he remains here. We are not responsible for his health. I suggest we vote on this," said Rolf, looking around at his fellow tourists.

The Italians and Dutch all started talking at once. Several started talking directly to Vulle at once.

"Please. Please. Please. Let me speak," shouted Vulle above the clatter of multiple voices.

The tourists gradually settled, stopped speaking, and waited for Vulle to speak.

"Mr. Rolf is not right about this," said Vulle. "There is nothing to be alarmed about. We can look after Henry here for a few days. Once the travel restrictions are over, we will transfer Henry to Tromsø, or Oslo, assuming he doesn't recover fully here. Everyone else can carry on as normal. There are no restrictions on us travelling around this area of countryside. You should just enjoy your trip and let me and my family take care of Henry."

"If you will not remove the American, then we can do this without you," said Rolf.

As Rolf spoke, Edo walked slowly from the back of the room to stand beside Vulle. His rifle was looped over his shoulder.

"Nobody will be moving Henry," said Vulle. "I am responsible for his safety. I will ensure that he is kept safe. He is too ill to move at present. The rest of you can stay away from his cabin. This is our land, and we look after all our guests, especially if they are ill."

"Ach. You will be in and out of his cabin," said Rolf. "And then you will be in and out of this cabin. For all we know, you are infecting us all as you speak. This is foolish nonsense. Henry Gibson is probably already doomed if he has a serious infection. Why should we risk the lives of the rest of us for one person?"

While Rolf was speaking, Sárá had walked quietly towards him. She stopped six feet away from him, facing him directly, and looked directly up at him. "You are speaking without knowledge," she said. "You are speaking from fear and ignorance. You have not gathered enough evidence to understand the balance of risks. There is no evidence that Henry has an infectious disease. There is much evidence that his illness is something very different. The Sami people have experience of illnesses like this. Some of us have a reaction to very cold weather that is more than just the coldness.

It can be a sickness of the blood. It is not something that can be passed between people. It is something we inherit from our parents. It is most likely that Henry has this type of blood sickness. Henry needs our help at this time. We have a tradition in the Sami culture to help people who are in need. We never turn people away when they are in need. After all, none of us know when we will need help, do we? We would offer help to you, Mr. Rolf, and to your wife, if you needed our help. I think there is a similar tradition in many other cultures. We are helping Henry, and I am confident that he will soon be much better. We will make sure that he does not affect your health. You need not worry about this. You can still enjoy your arctic safari without taking any responsibility for Henry. My daddy is right about this."

Rolf stared at the little girl standing before him. At first, his mouth opened, but nothing came out. Then his mouth curled with contempt. "I have nothing to learn from you," he said. "You are just a child. A little girl without any authority here. You know nothing. You should not interfere in the business of the adults. Vulle, tell your daughter to leave this matter to the adults."

Sárá interrupted Rolf. Her voice was quiet, calm, and level. She stood her ground, and her small hands closed by her sides into tiny fists. There was a compulsion about such a small, young person commanding the room. Despite his comments, Rolf stopped talking and listened.

"This is not a matter of age," she said slowly. "The fact that I am younger than you, or that you are an old man and I am a girl, makes no difference to this matter. I have greater knowledge than you about Henry's health. I have travelled with him and observed the pattern of his illness directly. I speak from a position of knowledge and understanding, not fear.

"To suggest that Henry should be thrown out to fend for himself is surely to condemn him to death in these conditions. You shame your family and your country for suggesting this. This would be murder. Mr. Rolf, you must not tell us how to care for our guests. This is not your responsibility. While you are in our country, you must accept the decision of my daddy and mummy. You are our guest as well, and you must respect us."

Once again Rolf appeared speechless. His mouth opened, and then closed, without any sound coming out. Finally he found his words again. "How dare you speak to me like this. It is disgusting that a mere girl is allowed to order me around. Vulle, tell your daughter to be silent and to respect her elders. I insist that the children should be removed from the room so that we can make a decision about our own safety. This is a matter of life and death, not some childish game."

Rolf looked around the room for support from the Italian and Dutch tourists. This time nobody stood up or spoke. They all looked away from Rolf.

The three Dutch travellers stood.

"I think Vulle is right," said Christiaan. "Vulle is looking after the American. We are not in contact with him. We should just carry on with our safari. The American will recover soon."

Rolf looked up at Vulle. Vulle looked directly at Sárá, then at Rolf. He smiled slightly and raised his eyebrows but said nothing. Then the Italian children whispered to their parents and laughed together.

Rolf stood and started walking out of the meeting. His wife, Ulva, initially stayed seated. Rolf turned to her and spoke sharply in German. She hurriedly stood and followed him. They both walked out of the cabin without another word. The Italian family followed, talking loudly to their children. It seemed the Italians were debating the issue.

"So, we are still not restricted in our movements? We can take trips out to see the lights and the scenery?" said Christiaan from the Dutch group.

Vulle looked at Ánne with a slight smile on his face. "You are free to explore our beautiful winter wilderness," he said. "However, this evening, the evening before Christmas, we know this as *ruohtta*, Mr. Christiaan. This means 'the night.' It is the most dangerous evening of the Sami year. If you make too much noise, you can draw ghosts towards you. There is also a risk that if you wander far, you will be taken by Stallo, who is a troll. Stallo looks like a human. He is like a bad version of Santa Claus. He is partial to drinking the blood of tender Dutch tourists, or reindeer. We will leave a bucket of water out to quench his thirst. Hopefully, this will keep him away from our reindeer. But we cannot guarantee this. So you and your friends must be very careful today, Mr. Christiaan. If you see Stallo, run for your life."

The candles flickered, and shadows danced on the walls and ceilings. For a brief second, Christiaan and his two friends paused, with serious looks on their faces. Everyone in the room was silent. Sárá clamped a hand over her mouth.

Then a suppressed laugh escaped from Sárá's mouth. Vulle, Oskár, and Ánne also burst out laughing. The spell was broken. Christiaan smiled at his two friends, looking embarrassed.

"Ja. Ja. Certainly," said Vulle. "You must enjoy your stay here and take advantage of our wonderful country. Take full advantage of our beautiful land. We have insurance in case tourists are eaten by trolls."

Everton walked to Vulle, leaned forwards, and spoke quietly into Vulle's ear. Vulle nodded and put a hand on Everton's arm.

Sárá carried a tray with three glasses of beer to the table where Christiaan, Willem, and Yvette sat talking in Dutch. She placed the drinks carefully in front of each of them, taking care not to spill any beer. The three Dutch tourists ignored her and continued to talk in Dutch to each other, as if she were invisible. As she walked around their table, she watched Christiaan closely, examining his expression and listening to his tone.

Without any introduction, Sárá asked, "How are you enjoying our arctic camp. Mr. Christiaan?"

Christiaan stopped speaking midsentence and slowly turned to look at Sárá as if he were becoming aware of her existence for the first time. His expression changed from a frown to a smile, and he said, "Very good, Sárá. It is Sárá, isn't it? Yes, we are enjoying ourselves very much, thank you."

Christiaan turned back to face Willem. This was an act of dismissal.

Sárá was undaunted. "Excuse me for asking, but what do you do for work in Holland, Mr. Christiaan?" she said.

Again, Christiaan turned slowly to face Sárá. This time he didn't bother with a smile. "I work in pharmaceuticals. We all work in pharmaceuticals. I am a researcher at Amsterdam University of Applied Science. You are too young to understand, of course," he said.

"I am sure you are right. After all, I am only nine years old," said Sárá, beaming her most charming smile full force at Christiaan. "What does your research involve?"

Christiaan paused, swallowed, and blinked. "Tropane alkaloids. I research the effects of tropane alkaloids. Do you know what these are?" he said.

Sárá nodded and paused. For once, she appeared hesitant to reply. However, she quickly overcame her reluctance. "I think we did a project about this at school. I might be wrong, Mr. Christiaan, but I believe that the tropane alkaloids include plant-based substances like atropine and cocaine. I remember that some of these chemicals come from plants such as the sorcerer's tree and henbane. We have henbane in Norway. It grows in our southern counties. It is also known as stinking nightshade, which is not really such a nice name, but very descriptive. Did you know that Vikings and witches used henbane as a poison for hundreds of years?"

Christiaan looks surprised and annoyed. "Yes. Yes. I am sure you are right. But we are busy right now, so you just run along and tell one of your little stories to the English tourists. Be a good girl and don't interrupt us."

"Of course, Mr. Christiaan. I am sorry to disturb you," said Sárá sweetly. Smiling, she turned and walked back to the bar with her tray.

After the evening meal, Jean and Everton walked back to Henry's cabin with Vulle and his family. Henry was still immobile on his bunk bed. He had not eaten or drunk anything for almost a full day. It was midevening on Christmas Eve. Inside, the cabin was warm due to the wood burner. Outside, the sky was clear and velvety black. A thin mist drifted across the Camp Trollfjell forest clearing. Ignoring the humans around them, the reindeer continued their calm feast of lichen, clanking their bells and grunting as they chewed.

Vulle explained to Beth about the enforced delay in medical evacuation.

"This is very disappointing, Vulle," said Beth. "It feels as if we are being cut off by the medical services. As if we are not important. Just because some people are ill in New York. Henry could die here without any access to medical care." Tears streamed down her cheeks.

"While the medical services are out of range, we need to decide what to do about Henry's illness. He seems to suffer each time he travels in the cold air," said Vulle. "The roads are closed by the snow and by the authorities in Tromsø. It could be a couple of days before any travel by road is possible. Taking Henry back to Camp Arktis on a sled would be very difficult and risky for him. He would be outside in the cold for most of a day, or longer if the weather became difficult. Henry did seem to recover quite well when we warmed him up. We have no choice. We must keep him warm here for now and look after him as well as we can."

"I want to mention the elephant in the room," said Beth, with tears in her eyes. "This illness we heard about in the news is in New York. Henry and I travelled through New York. If it is some sort of serious infection, I understand that bleeding is a feature of some of these illnesses. Henry might have this infection and might be putting everyone else at risk, including your family, Vulle."

There was a pause. Nobody wanted to speak first.

After half a minute, Ánne spoke. "I have some training as a nurse. I have worked in our hospitals from time to time. We have all been together for almost three days so far, yet only Henry has been ill. You have been with Henry since you travelled through New York, perhaps five days ago, and you have no symptoms.

It is very likely that some of us would be suffering symptoms by now if Henry had any contagious infection. Yet we are all well. I don't think this is an infection that Henry has."

"And in any case," said Jean, "we are all infected already if Henry has something contagious. We can't take this back now. We have an obligation to help Henry as much as possible."

"Thank you so much, Jean. You are very kind. You are all very kind. Henry would thank you all if he were awake," said Beth.

Sárá and Oskár were both talking quietly to each other in Sami. Sárá turned to her mother and said something, also in Sami. Ánne nodded in agreement with Sárá.

"While we cannot get medical services, Sárá might be able to help Henry," said Ánne.

Beth looked at Sárá and smiled. "How exactly do you mean?"

"Sárá has a…gift. A talent. She has some instincts for healing. We call people like Sárá *noaidi*. This means shaman or healer in English."

Beth was silent for a few seconds and looked from Ánne to Sárá and then back again.

"How old are you again, honey?" said Beth to Sárá.

"I will be ten years old next birthday," said Sárá in her perfect, slightly American English accent, smiling at Beth.

"How could you know what's wrong with my Henry?" said Beth.

"We Sami people have known about a…condition that affects some people in cold weather. It is different from the normal effect of the cold. Some people have a disorder of blood that can affect them if they get cold suddenly, even if they use warm clothes," said Sárá.

Jean and Everton watched this conversation with raised eyebrows. An almost-ten-year-old girl, speaking with the confidence and authority of an experienced doctor.

"How do you know that Henry has this blood condition?" said Beth.

Sárá and Ánne looked at each other for a few seconds. Vulle smiled and watched his young daughter.

"Some of this can be known by signs you can see easily. Henry's eyes have a slight yellow colour. The skin under his nails has a slight blue colour. These are signs of the underlying blood conditions. You already noticed that he was bleeding, in his water and from his stomach, when we stopped in the mountains. But what I am talking about is more than just the physical signs of illness. I sometimes get a sense of things. I sometimes get a feeling about the nature of an illness and the right solution. It is not always there. But when it comes, it is usually right. Even I don't really understand where it comes from," said Sárá.

"Well, I can see what you mean about Henry's hands and eyes," said Beth. "But how do you know this when you are not yet ten years old?"

Sárá took Beth's hand and looked into her eyes. "Are you Christian, Beth?"

"Henry and I are both Christians," said Beth.

"Good. You believe in some things that are not fully understood by modern science. This is common in the world. There are many things that are not yet explained by our science and medicine," said Sárá. "Indeed, it is an important part of the scientific and medical way of thinking to accept that there are many unknown things in the physical world. Sometimes we must try to understand problems with the…spiritual world…or the world of psychology, if you prefer. Accepting there are many unknown things, and keeping an open mind about these, is a strength. It is a good thing to know when to use physical healing and when to use spirit healing."

"So, you are saying you know these things because of spirits or religion. Are you saying you are a faith healer? Do you think that Henry can be healed by your faith?" said Beth.

"I am not quite sure of this thing you call faith healing," said Sárá. "After all, I cannot give Henry belief or faith, can I? Henry already has his own beliefs, and I have my own beliefs. When I say that I can sometimes sense things, I accept that everything we know, we have to learn through our senses. Even our knowledge of stars in the sky must be learned by what we see through telescopes or on computer screens. So we learn to trust our senses. In the same way, I can *feel* whether things are right or wrong. I trust those feelings. I suppose you can say I believe those feelings. Sometimes the feelings allow me to help heal some sick people.

"I have a good example. We learn in school about your English doctor, Edward Jenner. He was taught at his medical school, 'Don't think, try.' This was an instruction from his teachers to be empirical. He noticed that those who caught cowpox could not catch smallpox. He believed what his senses told him, even though there was no medical explanation for this at the time. He tried vaccinating people with cowpox, and he created the first vaccine, saving millions of lives. Well, I believe Dr. Jenner was right to try out his idea.

"Your famous Mr. Darwin is another good example. He wanted to train as a Christian priest at first, but then he decided he was more interested in observing nature. From his observations of different species, he had a *feeling* about how animals change over time, and he discovered evolution. In one of his notebooks, he drew the first branching tree of evolution and wrote, 'I think...' He did not write 'I know.' He was trusting his senses and making direct deductions but always keeping an open mind.

"After observing plants growing in his monastery, the famous friar, Mr. Mendel, had a similar *feeling* about how sweet peas change and deduced how genetic inheritance works.

"Well, I, too, believe the evidence that my senses receive. I believe it when I see people healing. One day our clever scientists will be able to explain how this healing works. Until then, I am happy to help where I can.

"My mother knows how to give injections or take blood from people. She has been trained to do this as a nurse. But I am different. I get a feeling, or perhaps I see signs unconsciously that make me know whether treatments will work. I sometimes feel very confident about these things, and mostly I am right. I think that my teachers and scientists call this being empirical," said Sárá with a broad smile.

Vulle and Ánne stood silently watching their daughter. They could hardly breathe with pride.

"Honey, you are so sweet. And you know such a lot for such a little lady. I want to thank you for what you say," said Beth, looking at Henry. "I don't know if you are right or wrong, but I am very glad that you are here to help Henry. I know you mean well. I think Henry would be very grateful if he could hear you now."

Beth leaned forwards and hugged Sárá tightly.

Everton looked at Jean with raised eyebrows. Jean shook her head and smiled back.

"What do you think about what Sárá has told me, from your training in nursing?" said Beth, looking at Ánne.

"I think that the Sami people use words that are different from the medical words that modern doctors use," said Ánne. "But I think that often they mean the same thing, or they are trying to solve the same problem. The Sami are describing processes with less scientific knowledge, but they still understand many of the underlying causes of illness. This is especially true for illnesses in our land, which have unique features. This knowledge has been acquired over thousands of years. Sami healers have found solutions to problems that are sometimes very effective by experimenting. Modern doctors admit they do not understand the natural triggers that start many illnesses or end these illnesses. Shaman healing cannot provide antibiotics or anaesthetics. However, sometimes Sami shaman healing can achieve similar ends using…spiritual…or psychological means. As long as the patient gets better, it doesn't really matter how this is achieved. Sárá sometimes has been able to help people. I don't know how she does it, but I am pleased when she succeeds."

"And in Henry's case, other than keeping him warm and feeding him, if he starts eating again, there is nothing else we can do at present, is there?" said Beth. "We are trapped by our circumstances. Events have conspired to block any access to conventional medical help. I have no choice but to stay here with Henry and hope for the best."

Beth turned back to Sárá and said, "What do you think we should do to make Henry better?"

"If you allow me, I will try to help Henry. This might stop the…*poison* that is hurting his blood. I would not do this without your permission. Without your permission, I could not help Henry. My influence would not have good effect," said Sárá.

There was a pause as Beth looked at each of the adults present. Jean nodded and smiled at Beth.

"OK, honey," said Beth. "You do what you can for Henry. I'm sure it won't hurt. And when the roads open and we are allowed, we will get Henry to a hospital for help, if he still needs it."

Sárá left the cabin and returned to the large lavvu in which her family were staying. She collected a backpack and returned to Henry's cabin. Sárá sat on Henry's bunk bed, opened the backpack, and took out a small leather pouch. From the pouch, she took out a small, smooth egg-shaped stone, about the size of her palm. She then took out a small drum made from a bowl of wood and measuring little more than six inches across. Hide was stretched across the bowl, and it was decorated with various black symbols. Next, she took out a single drumstick carved from bone. She opened one of Henry's hands, placed the stone in Henry's limp palm, and closed Henry's fingers around the stone. She picked up the drum, closed her eyes, breathed in deeply, and started tapping the drum lightly and regularly with the drumstick.

Vulle beckoned to Beth, Jean, and Everton to leave Sárá with Henry in the bedroom. Silently, they followed Vulle out of the room.

"Thank you for helping Henry," Beth said to Vulle. "I hope this works, because there is nothing else we can do."

"You are most welcome, Beth. I hope Sárá will be successful. Time will tell," said Vulle.

As they all waited, Vulle spoke to Everton and Jean. "Thank you for your help, Everton. And yours, Jean," said Vulle. "We must keep the hot heads cool. I am sure things will be much better within a day or two."

"What is Sárá doing with her drum?" said Jean.

"The drum is a rare object," said Vulle. "Many of our Sami drums were burned by the Christians in the seventeenth century. Some Sami believe that drums can be used by shamans to help them travel to the spirit world. The first Christians to arrive told us we were devil worshipping. There were witch trials, and many of our noaidi, our shamans, were decapitated and burned at the stake also. Of course, this just made our shamans hide. This drum has been in my family for many generations. Eventually the Christians accepted our beliefs, and we also accepted theirs. We didn't have to burn their priests at the stake in order to see that some of their beliefs were valid. Some of our drums are even decorated with Christian symbols. Sárá now uses the drum when she needs it. I don't know how it works, or even if it works. I don't really understand it. But then there are many things I don't understand. It doesn't mean they are wrong. I am happy for Sárá to follow her instincts. I have found that they are usually right."

Sárá stayed with Henry for over an hour. Eventually her soft drumming stopped, and she emerged from the bedroom, carrying her backpack. "I think I have spoken to Henry in another place. He told me he wants to return, and I saw him start his journey back here…and back to health. I am confident that he will improve, because this is what he wants. I think we just need to be patient and to keep him warm," she said.

She then turned to Everton. "While I was helping Henry, I also saw you, Mr. Everton, and Daddy, in a cabin in the forest. There were some flying…spirits…over the cabin. You had found some form of…treasure in the cabin. Or something else important or valuable, but not quite treasure. I cannot be sure."

Everton and Vulle looked at each other.

"Well, thank you for letting us know about that, Sárá," said Everton. "We will watch out for treasure in any cabins we visit."

Finally, Sárá turned to Vulle. "Daddy, I also saw us both in my dream. We were on ice, but it was not safe ice. We were facing danger together, and we needed help from the spirits. There was death, very close to us. The spirits told me that they would help us when we were in danger."

Vulle lifted Sárá and hugged her tightly. "I will protect you from danger, little one. I hope the spirits will do this too, of course, but even if they don't, I will not allow you to come to any harm."

Later that evening Jean and Everton were back in their cabin, lying on their beds. The cabin was warm enough for them to have removed their thermal undergarments. Outside it was misty and fiercely cold, making the warmth of the cabin even more comfortable.

"Christmas Day tomorrow. This is a most unusual Christmas. I could not have expected many of the things that have happened to us since we arrived here," said Jean.

"You are not wrong. What did you make of young Sárá today?" said Everton.

"Well, she is certainly a very…intuitive young lady," said Jean. "She is bright as a button. And most of all, she is very courageous. To challenge the bully Rolf like that in front of all the adults was very brave. She ended up being the leader of the entire camp for those few moments. She made Rolf look petty and stupid. Vulle and Ánne have a wonderful daughter. She seems to have very good social awareness, which makes her unusually confident with adults. Her confidence seems contagious to those with whom she speaks. I was very impressed with her description of Jenner's invention of vaccination, not to mention Darwin and

Mendel, all based on observations and deduction. The Norwegian education system, or perhaps the Sami education system, is clearly doing something right with their youth. She is clearly absorbing knowledge like a dry sponge."

"Yes, she is quite remarkable," said Everton. "And I am sure there is a good explanation for her psychological effect on others," said Everton. "She is clearly a bright star. But what do you think about the spirit stuff that she and Vulle talk about?"

"If you are asking me if I think there are supernatural forces that will cure Henry, then no, I don't think so. I don't believe in supernatural forces. But are there features of illnesses that are not understood by contemporary psychologists and doctors? Yes, of course there are. Are there some illnesses that can be helped by psychological therapies? Yes, of course. Indeed, that is the whole ethos underpinning my profession, clinical psychology," said Jean. "What do you think of the spiritual aspect of this?"

"Sárá is very convincing when she speaks. I am surprised by how we all accepted her offer to help heal Henry. I suppose it was because we are unable to access conventional medical services. I don't know what to make of the treasure that Vulle and I are going to find, or the danger that Sárá dreamed about. I think that part was just imagination," said Everton.

"I wasn't sure either. Sárá has a charismatic personality," said Jean. "Some people are born with the talent of inspiring others. Religious and political leaders have had this talent for thousands of years. By the way, what was that secret whisper you passed to Vulle, back in the dining cabin?"

"Oh, nothing really. I just reassured him that I was with him in terms of protecting Henry from the crazy old coot, Rolf, who wanted to throw Henry out in the snow," said Everton.

"Did you notice that Edo had his rifle with him during the meeting? Was that a deliberate and serious statement he was making when he walked around to join Vulle?" said Jean.

"Mmm. I think Vulle and Edo were deliberately making a point about where the power, and the responsibility, lies out here in the frozen north. We depend on the survival skills of our Sami hosts. They are our protectors while we are here. So we must accept that they have ultimate authority while we are disconnected from the cities and modern sources of authority. We are on a tourist holiday, of course. But we are also in a place that is very hostile to human life. We must be careful to follow the advice of our hosts. I am glad that Edo had the rifle and not Rolf," said Everton.

"You and Vulle seem thick as thieves since your trip on the sled. Wolf spirits, magic lights in the sky. You seem to have joined up as a fully-paid-up member of the Vulle wolf spirit fan club. If I didn't know better, I would think you and he had been wolf-friends for years," said Jean.

"I like Vulle. His family have been very kind to us, and to Henry and Beth. This trip has turned out quite different from my expectations since we left Camp Arktis. Without Vulle and his family, we might have had quite a difficult time. Henry might have died if we had tried to return to Camp Arktis," said Everton.

"It certainly isn't just another sand, sun, and sea holiday. I suppose that is part of the charm of travelling to the arctic in the middle of winter. It requires very specialized skills and knowledge to survive in this latitude and to herd reindeer in a country with multiple large predators. We've been in Norway—or is it Finland now?—for three days. It seems like three weeks," said Jean.

"And Christmas Day in a few hours. Let's see what treasure Santa brings," said Everton.

Henry's Dream

HENRY OPENED HIS EYES and blinked several times rapidly. Bright light blinded him for a brief moment. As his vision acclimatised to the bright light, he looked around.

He was lying on soft grass, under the branches of a large ash tree. The sun was shining brightly, but it was low on the horizon. It was warm. Far too warm for his multiple layers of thick winter clothing.

Henry pushed himself up to a sitting position, with the intention of taking some of his warm clothes off. He had a feeling that he was still wearing thick layers of warm clothes, double gloves, and sturdy winter walking boots. He was surprised to see that he was only wearing a light summer shirt, with short sleeves, light cotton trousers, and his summer walking shoes.

Somehow, I have been moved while I was asleep, he thought. *And someone has dressed me in summer clothes. How has the weather changed so quickly? Who moved me? Where is Beth?*

None of his fellow travellers appeared to be within sight. Beth was nowhere to be seen. Almost everything that he remembered had disappeared—dogs, cabins, snow, everything.

This is odd, he thought. *I feel as if I am in an episode of* Doctor Who, *or on the holodeck in* Star Trek. *I've been transported to an alternative time, place, and dimension. Perhaps I have been ill for a long time and I am convalescing. Perhaps my illness has caused amnesia. If this is real, then I should be alarmed and worried. But I don't seem to be. I feel quite calm. Actually, I feel great. Better than I have felt in a long time. That in itself is odd. I must be dreaming. Get a grip, Henry. Even if this is a dream, you should explore and find out what is going on here.*

He stood and turned a full circle, taking in his surroundings.

The tree under which he had been sleeping soared above him. It was a gigantic ash tree. It was the biggest tree he had ever seen. It sent out three enormous roots, which ran above the grass for tens of metres before sinking into the soil. A grassy clearing spread in every direction for several kilometres. Occasional similar large trees dotted the grassy plain, and a dense forest of mature trees encircled the plain. In all directions, beyond the forest, rose high mountains with snow-covered peaks, shimmering in the sunlight.

This is a bit chocolate boxy, thought Henry. *If I had imagined a beautiful grassy glade surrounded by a forest, encircled by stunning mountains, it would look just like this. I am pretty sure this is my imagination at work here. Am I dreaming? Come to think of it, am I dreaming about dreaming now? These thoughts are getting a bit circular. I hope I remember all this when I wake. This will be a really juicy dream to tell Beth about. Of course, I normally forget dreams pretty quickly. This is always a pain. Even very interesting dreams just evaporate within minutes. Hang on. I'm getting sidetracked about dreams and forgetting to be aware of the actual dream I'm in. Is it possible to practise mindfulness during a dream? I wonder.*

A large bird, perhaps an eagle, was circling above the tree. As he watched it, the bird landed in the upper branches and looked down at him. Although the eagle was hundreds of feet above him, he could see details of the bird's feathers clearly.

My vision is better than it has been in years, he thought. *This must have been what it was like to see when I was a child. I had forgotten how clear the world looks. I wonder if that eagle is thinking that I might be his lunch.*

Henry walked away from the tree a couple of hundred metres and turned to look back. There were no signs of any human habitations in the large clearing. The large ash tree was at the centre of the clearing. The surrounding forest, and the ring of mountains farther out, seemed to isolate and enclose the clearing. It was almost as if the mountains were a protective ring around the clearing.

Without hearing anyone approach, Henry became aware of someone standing behind him and turned sharply.

A man stood watching Henry, about ten paces away. The man stared at Henry with a slight smile. Two ravens perched on the man's shoulders. The ravens looked from Henry to the man and then back again. Two wolves stood either side of the man, both standing very still and staring at Henry. The wolves were very large, the size of small reindeer. The man was tall, well over six feet, perhaps even more than seven feet. He was the tallest man that Henry had ever met, by far. The man had a long white beard and a tangle of long white hair, which made him appear even larger. His right eye was closed, perhaps even missing. But his left eye was bright, blue, and alert. Henry struggled to focus on exactly what the man wore. He seemed to be wearing a dark blue cloak with a silver clasp. Henry could see strange letters engraved on the clasp. It felt to Henry as if the man was wearing outdoor clothing under his cloak. Perhaps trousers, hiking boots, and a cotton shirt peeked out from the edges of the cloak. Henry was unsure. It was as if the man's clothing was a little blurred. The man held a wooden staff in his right hand, planted on the grass. The wooden staff was as tall as the man.

"Who called me?" asked the man. He spoke softly, but his deep, sonorous voice easily filled the clearing.

"I…er…I'm not entirely sure," said Henry. "I'm Henry. Henry Gibson. I've only just arrived here. Pleased to meet you, Mr…"

Henry stepped forwards and held out his hand. Both wolves growled, a low sound that came from deep within them.

The man stared at Henry's hand and stroked the head of one of his wolves. One of the ravens croaked. The man turned his head and looked at the raven as if he understood and nodded slightly.

Henry took a step back and lowered his hand. "Could I ask who you are and where we are?" he said.

"I have many names with your people. Too many to list. You can call me Grim," said the man.

"Right. Well, I am very pleased to meet you, Mr. Grim. Do you know where we are exactly? I don't seem to have a clear idea of this at present. I can't remember exactly how I got here. I just woke up under that ash tree."

"This place is called the Sacred Forest. Someone sent you here, and I heard their call. Who called me?" said the man.

"I can't really explain it," said Henry. "I'll tell you what I know. Perhaps you will understand it better than me. I have been travelling in Norway with my wife, Beth. We are from Florida in the United States. You may know that Florida is warm all year round. We were travelling by dogsled, to see the northern lights. We were taking a Christmas winter safari and planning to stay with a Sami family for a few days. I started to become ill for the past few days, on and off. Every time I went out in the cold, I became ill. The Sami family, with whom we were travelling, were trying to help me because we couldn't get medical services for some reason. There is some sort of infection outbreak, and travel restrictions are in place in England and America. A small girl named Sárá was trying to help me, I think. I was asleep most of the time. Sárá was talking to me and beating some kind of drum. She gave me a stone to hold. It was warm and seemed to be throbbing. Then I woke under that large ash tree."

Henry paused for breath. It made no sense to him. How would it make sense to Mr. Grim?

"Ah, Sárá called me," said Grim, nodding his head as if remembering something. He ignored Henry's story about illness and only seemed interested in Sárá. "I know this Sárá. We have spoken before. She has visited this place many times. She and I have spoken often. She is well known to my people. She is a great talker. But she listens as well. She talks to my people all the time in her world. I am sure we will speak again soon."

Both of the ravens raised their beaks and emitted loud, gurgling croaks.

It sounds like they are laughing, thought Henry.

"Yes, I expect so," said Henry, not at all certain about this. "So, you already know Sárá. What exactly does Sárá speak to you about?"

The tall man thought for a few seconds before replying. "Sárá asks many questions. She talks to my ravens and wolves. She thinks I do not know this, but whatever she tells them, she tells me also. She is drinking in the knowledge of centuries. She pesters us all the time, doesn't she?" said Grim, ruffling the hair on the head of one of his wolves.

The two ravens again opened their beaks and emitted gurgling croaks. This time it seemed as if the ravens were gossiping to each other and to Grim. Henry couldn't understand what they were saying, but he felt that understanding of their language was only just outside his grasp. If only he could catch one or two words, he felt that the rest would be clear.

Grim smiled and chuckled. Henry felt a slight tremor in the ground as Grim laughed.

"I think that Sárá is just trying to help me at present," said Henry. "She might be misguided. But she genuinely seems to believe she can heal people. You can't fault her for trying to help others, I think. I don't imagine she is doing anyone any harm, even if she is mistaken. It does seem a little ridiculous, saying it out loud like this. A nine-year-old acting like a doctor or a counsellor. At any other time, I would think it was nonsense. But somehow it doesn't seem so weird with Sárá. I really must be dreaming all this. Do you think I am dreaming, Mr. Grim?"

Grim listened quietly to Henry and smiled. "You are wise to trust Sárá. Her years are misleading. And size is not everything. She is seeking true wisdom, as I do, and for this, we must respect her. But there is always a price for anything of value. She will pay her price as well," said Grim.

Henry looked into Grim's one open eye. Henry was over six feet tall, but Grim towered above him. Grim's eye was pale blue, the colour of the sky on a bright winter's day, when the frost is hard on the ground. In that one eye, Henry seemed to see the entire world, then the entire Milky Way, then galaxies stretching out infinitely into the vastness of space. At the same time, Henry seemed to see the smallest particle of the universe in fine detail, then the smallest part of the smallest particle, extending infinitely into the smallest possible piece of space. The sensation caused Henry to feel dizzy. It was as if he were falling into Grim's eye. As if Grim's eye were actually a deep hole from which there would be no return. Then, suddenly, Henry's view snapped back, and he blinked and saw Grim's face smiling back at him.

Henry blushed and looked away. He was reluctant to stare at Grim's single eye. He didn't want to offend Grim.

"I would be very grateful for any advice you can offer me. Do you know how I can get back to…to Camp Trollfjell? I really want to return to my wife, Beth. She will be very worried about me," said Henry.

"Walk with me," said Grim. He turned and started walking away from the ash tree, towards the encircling forest. The two wolves kept perfect pace beside Grim as he walked, and the ravens flew off his shoulders and circled above him, shouting the occasional croak to each other.

The invitation to walk with Grim did not appear to be optional, so Henry trotted alongside him, keeping a few paces from the wolves. At each step of Grim, the ground shook very slightly.

The two men walked in silence for several minutes towards the forest.

"Do you know how long I have been here?" said Henry, breaking the silence.

"Time is less certain in this place than on your world. Your stay here is not easily measured in the time from the world of men. It may be that you have been here for no time at all. It may also be that many centuries could pass before you return," said Grim.

Right. Well, that's totally clear, then, thought Henry. *I might get back to meet my great-great-grandchildren.*

"So, what exactly is this place?" said Henry, trying another line of enquiry.

"You might consider this place to be a meeting of ways. It is an in-between place for travellers moving between destinations," said Grim.

This is all rather vague, thought Henry. *Beth would be much better at this. She would start with open questions and then narrow down the questions to pin Mr. Grim down.*

"Elizabeth is waiting for your return. If you decide to return, she will be waiting for you," said Grim.

Well, that is spooky. This chap might be a mind reader, thought Henry. *I suppose that makes it more likely that this is a dream. If he is in my dream, then he is in my mind. There I go again, thinking about dreaming while I am dreaming.*

If Grim was reading Henry's mind, he ignored the last thought.

"I do want to return to…to Elizabeth. Yes, I definitely do want to go back. I would be very grateful if you could guide me as to the right direction, Mr. Grim?" said Henry.

"That is not why I was called," said Grim. "Sárá wants to help you. She is asking me, and others, how to help you. My raven Huginn brought her call to me. I have already replied to her. If you decide to return to the world of men, she will tell you what to do. She is good at telling people what to do."

Grim turned and looked at the ravens circling above them. One of the ravens gave a short croak, as if acknowledging Grim's comment.

"I see," said Henry, without really seeing at all.

"There is one answer that I will give you to take to Sárá, if you return. The answer to one of her questions lies in the Sacred

Forest. If you want to help Sárá, you should take this answer back to her," said Grim.

"Right. OK. But you say this is the Sacred Forest. So the answer lies here. I'll certainly try to remember to tell Sárá that, Mr. Grim. But I'm afraid I still have no idea how to get back," said Henry.

They were approaching the edge of the forest. Grim stopped walking, and his ravens settled on his shoulders again.

He turned to face Henry. "Henry, son of Gib, this is where our paths part," said Grim. He touched the head of one of his wolves. "We will meet again. I have asked my wolf Freki to protect Sárá. She will know him by another name, but she has already seen him. And Huginn's eyes will never be far from you and Sárá when you need them, as you travel. Farewell."

Grim turned towards the forest. His ravens flew up into the air again. He started walking away from Henry towards the edge of the forest, his wolves walking at his side. The trees and bushes seemed to part to allow him to enter, then closed together after he passed. Within a few paces, he and his animals disappeared between the trees.

Henry was left standing staring after Grim, at the thick vegetation.

I had better not enter this forest, he thought. *It looks pretty dense in there. I might not find my way out. I don't think that is my way back.*

Once again, Henry did not hear or see anyone approaching. But without any warning, a lady was standing next to him. She touched his arm gently, and he jumped.

"Whoa. Where did you spring from? This place is full of surprises," said Henry.

"You called me here, Henry," said the lady. "You wanted to ask me something. My name is Sárá."

She was almost as tall as Henry, just under six feet. She had long, white-blond hair and bright blue eyes. She wore a hide tunic and skirt. Her feet were bare.

Henry stared at her face. It was familiar, yet he was sure he had never met her before.

"You are Sárá?" said Henry. "The same Sárá who is helping me back...back there, wherever that is?"

"I will try to help you in any way I can," said the lady.

"OK," said Henry. "I'm getting used to this. People appearing and disappearing. Strange places. Strange weather too. If you are the same Sárá as the little girl back in Camp Trollfjell, then what is all this about, and when did you grow up?"

"Only you can answer those questions, Henry," said the lady who might have been the same Sárá he had met as a child. "What do you think is going on?"

Henry paused and considered this question. "Well, it might all be a dream," he said. "I might be dreaming based on mythology from Norse and Sami cultures. I read a bit about this stuff before coming out on this trip. Sárá and Vulle have been talking about this with us. I might have fused and confused legends and myths, fitting these legends into a pattern that fits with my current illness. I might really still be lying on a bunk bed, in a cabin, in Norway, or Finland, with a fever, and with Beth sitting near me wondering why I don't wake up."

"Yes, that is always possible, of course," said Sárá. "A fever, or a misplaced fish bone, might disturb the mind sufficiently to induce delirium and delusions. However, the nature of a dream, or delirium, is that one cannot distinguish reality from imagination at the time of the dream. Only in retrospect can perspective be gained. The Greek philosopher Plato described this in his allegory of the cave. To someone who only sees shadows, shadows are the only reality. Perspective is everything. So the best course is to address reality as it presents itself to you now. If you later wake and perceive all this to be a dream, then no harm can come of the assumption."

"I suppose you're right. I might even have said that myself. In fact, if this is my dream, in effect I did say it myself," said Henry. "Do you think I could just choose to wake up? Right now? Back in Camp Trollfjell?"

"I cannot say what you can or cannot do, Henry. You are where you choose to be. We are all free to make our choices. You control what you can do. Our life is the sum of all our choices. Do you want to recover from your illness, Henry? Or would you prefer to remain here and take a different journey onwards? Your will is paramount in this. You have all options before you. But remember, whatever path you choose, other paths will be closed to you. Once you decide some things, you cannot reverse some of those decisions," said Sárá.

"OK. If I can control this, let's say I have decided to go back. To wake up. To return to where I came from. To recover from whatever I was suffering from. Yes, I have definitely decided this. I want to return to Beth, to Norway, to Camp Trollfjell. Now, just how do I make all this happen? What choices do I make, and how do I make them?" said Henry.

"It is your decision, Henry. Not mine. How you choose to do this is entirely for you to decide," said Sárá.

Henry thought back to his time in Camp Trollfjell. *I arrived by dogsled. Perhaps I need another dogsled to get back? Or an all-terrain vehicle. Or a helicopter? Heck, since this is my dream, why don't I just dream up a helicopter and fly right out of here?*

"Sárá, please, could you get me some form of vehicle in which I can travel back to Camp Trollfjell? If you know what a helicopter is, that would be perfect," said Henry.

"Let's walk a little," said Sárá, holding out her hand to indicate one direction.

Henry turned in the direction Sárá was pointing. There was now a clear path leading between the silver birch trees that formed most of the surrounding forest.

I don't think that path was there when I last looked, thought Henry.

Henry and Sárá started to walk down the forest path. The grass and moss under their feet was soft and springy. After a short period, they emerged at the edge of a lake. The lake was several kilometres across. A few hundred metres from them, a bridge spanned the lake, running to the far shore. The bridge was low, only rising to about five or six metres above the lake and supported every twenty metres by transparent pillars that sank into the lake. There was no rail on either side of the bridge.

Sárá led Henry towards the bridge. As they approached it, Henry realised that the bridge seemed to be made from a transparent material.

"This bridge seems to be made from glass. Who built this?" said Henry.

"It is not glass. It is more like ice in your world. But not quite the same as ice," said Sárá.

Sárá led Henry onto the bridge. Henry tested the surface carefully with his shoes. It looked as if it was slippery. However, he found it to be firm underfoot. His shoe did not slip at all on it. He stopped and ran his hand over the surface. It did not feel cold like ice. It was smooth but not so smooth that it was slippery.

Henry followed Sárá onto the bridge, and they started to walk over the lake.

As they walked farther onto the bridge, Henry became aware that there was a figure standing on the bridge ahead of them.

"Who is that?" said Henry.

"We are going to meet someone who wants to stop me from helping you," said Sárá. "Don't be worried. Help surrounds us and will always come when we need it."

As they closed the distance between them and the figure, Henry saw that it was a tall person, probably over six feet tall. It appeared to be a woman. She had long, greasy black hair. She wore a long garment that reached to the floor. It was torn and ragged.

The woman ahead just stood still in the middle of the bridge as they approached. Sárá held up a hand when they approached to ten metres from the woman, and they stopped.

Henry was close enough to see that the woman had a strange face. Her mouth and nose appeared more like the snout of a dog than a human.

As they stood apart, the woman sniffed in their direction. "You cannot pass, and you will not return to your world," said the woman.

"You have no power to stop us. Stand aside and let us pass. We have no quarrel with you, Padnakjunne," said Sárá.

The woman reached behind her and pulled out a long, curved knife. The blade glinted in the sunlight. She held the blade directly in front of her, pointing directly at Sárá.

Sárá stepped forwards, and the woman also stepped forwards. As they approached each other, the woman swung the knife swiftly towards Sárá's face. Sárá moved equally swiftly to dodge the knife. The two women came to a halt again. A small area of blood appeared on Sárá's left ear, and blood started to drip onto her tunic and onto the bridge.

Henry wanted to help Sárá and was about to step forwards when he became aware that there was someone else next to him. He looked to his right, and a large wolf was standing facing Sárá and the woman.

The wolf did not acknowledge Henry. Instead, it loped calmly towards the tall woman.

As the wolf advanced, Sárá stepped back a couple of paces.

The tall woman became aware of the wolf and turned to point her knife at it. The wolf continued to walk towards the woman, perfectly calmly, as if the knife did not exist. As the wolf reached the woman, she lunged at it with her knife. The wolf easily dodged her clumsy attempts to strike with her knife. He circled the woman, jumping at her intermittently as she became unbalanced and nipping her arm or leg. This happened repeatedly for two or three minutes. The tall woman became more and more clumsy and exhausted. Despite her attempts, she was unable even to scratch the wolf. It was just too skilled and fast for her.

Throughout this contest, Sárá stood and watched the wolf. Henry stood and watched Sárá watching the fight.

The woman stopped moving for a few seconds. She was breathing heavily, and blood was dripping from several small wounds on her arms and legs where the wolf had nipped her. She stared at the wolf, gathered her strength, and made one last desperate lunge with her knife.

The wolf moved quickly. He only moved a few inches. It was just sufficient. The knife cut through air yet again. The woman was unbalanced and fell. She toppled over the edge of the bridge but just managed to catch the lip of it with her free hand. She hung over the lake, breathing heavily.

Sárá stepped towards the woman and took hold of her wrist with both hands. "Drop your knife. Grab my hands. I will help you climb back. I have no quarrel with you. You can go on your way," said Sárá.

The woman ignored Sárá's pleas and swung the knife with her free hand towards Sárá's face.

Sárá released the woman's wrist and stepped back. The knife whistled past her nose without causing any harm. The effort released the woman's hold on the bridge, and she fell silently into the lake.

Henry and the wolf both advanced to look over the edge.

The woman sank silently into the lake and disappeared from view.

Sárá turned towards the wolf and held out both of her hands. "Thank you for your help. Once again, you and your master are with me when I need you," said Sárá.

The wolf stepped towards Sárá. Sárá crouched and rubbed the wolf's face with both hands. Sárá and the wolf touched noses and stared into each other's eyes.

Blood was dripping slowly from a cut on Sárá's left ear.

The wolf moved its nose and sniffed at Sárá's injury. He breathed on her left ear, the cut disappeared, and the blood stopped dripping.

Henry watched as the wolf turned and walked back along the bridge in the direction from which they had come.

"I think we can cross now. I doubt that there will be any more obstacles in our way," said Sárá.

Henry could not think of anything to say. He was astonished by the entire episode. Henry and Sárá walked together in silence for several minutes, along the bridge, towards the far shore of the lake.

"You mentioned that the wolf had helped you before," said Henry eventually. "When did you two meet?"

"It is not easy to answer that question," said Sárá. "The concept of before and after don't apply in quite the same way as you would normally think. Suffice to say, we met, and we will meet, several times over my life, always as friends."

They walked on in silence.

As they stepped off the bridge and onto dry land, Sárá looked north, put two fingers in her mouth, and gave a loud and piercing whistle.

She is certainly a good whistler, thought Henry. *Not many ladies can whistle like that. In fact, not many guys can whistle like that.*

From the edge of the forest, several hundred metres away, an animal emerged and walked towards them. As it approached, Henry realised it was a reindeer with huge antlers. It was pulling a sleigh across the grass. It trotted up to Sárá and stopped. Sárá stroked its neck gently.

"Come and say hello, Henry. Don't worry. He is friendly with you. He already knows you, and you already know him. You just don't remember him at present. Be careful not to touch his antlers. Reindeer don't like you touching their antlers," said Sárá.

Henry approached the reindeer and stroked its neck. The reindeer looked at Henry and then back at Sárá.

"Hello there. You seem like a friendly fellow," said Henry to the reindeer.

Large golden eyes looked up at him.

There was silence for a few minutes as Sárá and Henry both stroked the reindeer. It was very peaceful. Henry was slightly tempted not to leave the clearing at all. *It might be great to stay here,* he thought. Then he remembered Beth.

"I think that you called the reindeer as a means for me to return to…to wherever I was before. And I assume I can travel in this sleigh," said Henry, more to himself than to Sárá.

"I didn't call him. You did, Henry," said Sárá.

"Of course. My dream, my whistle, my reindeer. So how do I get him to take me back?" said Henry.

"You already know that," said Sárá.

Henry looked at the reindeer and the sleigh. "OK. Since this is my dream, I make the rules. I can decide the route back," he said.

Henry climbed onto the sleigh and took hold of the reins. "Mush," he said, and he shook the reins.

Nothing happened. The reindeer stood waiting and turned its head to look at him. It seemed to be saying, "What exactly are we waiting for?"

Henry realised he could not speak to a reindeer, and he knew no commands for reindeer. Sárá was still watching him.

He sat thinking for a few minutes. "Sárá, I am going back to Beth. Thank you for taking the time to talk to me and to help me. I hope we meet again. If you are the same Sárá that I met in…in my world, as a little girl, I will thank you again when I get back," he said.

"You are very welcome, Henry," said Sárá.

Without prompting, the reindeer started to walk towards the large ash tree at the centre of the clearing, under which Henry had awoken.

Henry suddenly remembered something. He had to tell Sárá something that Grim had told him. He turned his head to shout back the message from Grim. Sárá was nowhere to be seen.

As they approached the tree, the reindeer, sleigh, and Henry seemed to reduce in size, or the tree started enlarging. An opening appeared in the ground where one of the tree roots disappeared downwards. The root seemed to change into something that looked like a path or a road. The reindeer calmly stepped onto the road and started trotting down into the ground. The pace increased, and the road seemed to race under the sleigh. The ground on either side passed in a blur, even though the reindeer was only trotting gently. It looked more like a night sky full of stars streaming past on either side.

CHAPTER 8

Henry Wakes

THE GROUND SLID PAST the sleigh on all sides at a dizzying pace. The speed they were travelling was so fast that Henry couldn't even focus on the road beneath them. Yet Henry had felt no acceleration forces. Henry rubbed his forehead and closed his eyes.

As he was rubbing his forehead, he realised that he was not actually rubbing his forehead at all. Someone else was doing this. Someone was also talking to him.

He opened his eyes. Beth was sitting next to him, stroking his hair and smiling at him.

"You're back with us, Henry. I thought you were gone for good. You gave me a mighty fright. I guess you had me fooled all along. Merry Christmas, Henry. It's Christmas Day," said Beth, and she planted a kiss on Henry's cheek.

Henry sat up and blinked. He was still in the cabin at Camp Trollfjell, lying on a bed.

"I need to tell you about my dream quickly, Beth. It's disappearing from my memory already. I think I had a dream. I went to a place in the mountains. It was summertime. I woke under a large tree and met some people there. I met a guy called Mr. Grim and a lady called Sárá there. We walked around for a while and had a good chat about things. There was an eagle, and some ravens and wolves. But they were all magic animals who could understand me. After a while, I decided to come back here. I came back on a magic reindeer sleigh. I think…" said Henry.

"Hush, Henry. You lie back and rest. I'll get the others," said Beth.

Beth put her coat and boots on. It was minus twenty Celsius outside. She crunched through the newly fallen snow, under the lights of the Camp. Ten minutes later she returned with Sárá, Vulle, Everton, and Jean. By the time they returned, Henry was out of bed, sitting at the table in his cabin, with a glass of water in his hand.

Beth sat next to Henry at the table while the others stood behind her.

"Henry, it's good to see you sitting up and awake. You have had a good sleep," said Vulle.

"It's nice to be back. I am so hungry, I could eat a whole turkey. I hope Christmas dinner is still on," said Henry.

Vulle laughed. "We will have some special food today. There are not many turkeys wandering around Camp Trollfjell, but we will feed you well. How do you feel?" he said.

"I feel fantastic. Never felt better. I feel I could climb a mountain, perhaps after I have a bite to eat. But first I need to tell you what I remember about my dream," said Henry.

"OK, Henry. Tell us all what you wanted to say about your dream," said Beth.

Henry looked at the faces staring down at him. "I'm not sure. The memory is fading for what I dreamed. Yes. I can remember some of it. There was a tree. A huge tree. I woke up under the tree. It was warm. Summertime, I think. I saw an eagle, and I met a man, Mr. Grim, who had two ravens with him and two huge wolves. He called himself Mr. Grim. Oh, I already said that. A large fellow, with a wooden staff and a blue cloak. We had a good talk, but I can't remember much about what he said."

Vulle spoke to Sárá in Sami, and Sárá left the cabin.

"I have asked Sárá to get you some soup and bread. She will be back soon. You need to build up your strength again," said Vulle. "What do you remember of our journey from Camp Arktis to Camp Trollfjell?"

Henry scratched his head. "I don't remember much, really. I think I remember someone telling stories about dogs and sleds and snow. I remember being chased by some wolves. Then someone was ill. I think it might have been me."

Sárá came back carrying a tray on which she brought a bowl of steaming fish soup and some flatbread.

As he ate, between mouthfuls, Henry started to remember fragments of his dream.

"I am starting to remember now. The chap Mr. Grim told me that the answer was in the Sacred Forest. For some reason, I wanted an answer to something. He told me that the place I went was the Sacred Forest, but the answer to the question was also in the Sacred Forest. The answer to what, though? I have no idea. But he did tell me to tell Sárá this, about the Sacred Forest," he said, turning to look at Sárá.

Sárá said something to Vulle in Sami.

"Yes, I remember now—you were in the dream, Sárá. At least someone with your name was there. But you were much older, an adult. We walked on a glass bridge over a lake. You—or rather Sárá—were attacked by a weird lady with a face like a dog. A wolf arrived and helped us. The dog lady slipped and fell into the lake. The Sárá in the dream helped me get back from the forest to here. This will sound completely mad, I know. The Sárá in the dream called a reindeer, with a sleigh, and I rode in the sleigh. The reindeer came back by riding on the root of the big tree, which became a sort of tunnel. I know this is quite bizarre, but it all seemed very reasonable at the time. I guess that's the nature of dreams," said Henry.

He stopped talking and concentrated on his soup.

"Can you describe this man Mr. Grim?" said Sárá.

"Yes. I think. Yes, he was very tall," said Henry. "At least a foot taller than me. He had a blue cloak and a wooden staff. His eye was blue, but one eye was missing. And he had two ravens who sat on his shoulders most of the time. He also came with two wolves who walked at his side. Now I'm starting to remember. He said one of his ravens was keeping an eye on you and that you talked a lot to the raven. And the ravens laughed about that."

Sárá smiled and looked at her father, who smiled and nodded back.

"And he also said that one of his wolves would protect someone…I think he said the wolf would protect you as well, Sárá," said Henry. "It's a bit of a blur now."

"We will leave now to have a shower and get ready for our Christmas celebrations," said Vulle. "We have some great food for this afternoon, and we can talk about your dreams. Keep warm, and don't forget to put on all your layers, even walking between your cabin and the dining cabin."

"If I could get some more of this excellent fish soup, I would be very happy," said Henry.

Vulle looked at Sárá, and Sárá whisked away the tray and went to get another bowl.

Vulle, Jean, and Everton left the cabin to allow Henry a chance to freshen up. Henry had a warm shower. By the time he was finished, Sárá had brought another bowl of soup, which he devoured rapidly. He was making up for lost time.

It was late morning on Christmas Day. The dark sky was clear, and the snow was deep on the ground. The Milky Way stood out in the sky. Everton, Jean, and Vulle walked back towards their cabin through the thick, dry snow. As they walked, Jean spoke. "Vulle, I wanted to tell you about something I heard this afternoon. I speak a little Dutch, so I can understand some of what Christiaan and his friends are saying. I overheard them talking together. They seemed to be saying, 'It's going well,' or possibly 'We're doing well.' They also said something like, 'We are on schedule,' or perhaps, 'It's all on schedule.' I can't be absolutely sure. They all seemed very pleased with themselves. Then Christiaan said something odd. I am sure he said, 'We must not allow the American to interfere with our plans.' I thought this was quite callous and cold, talking about Henry and his illness. I was surprised. I don't know what it means really. Perhaps nothing, but I wanted to tell you just in case."

Vulle looked at Everton for several seconds, then said, "Thank you for telling me, Jean. I am not sure what this means also, but I think you were right to tell me. I will keep an eye on these young Dutch people."

"Thank you, Vulle," said Jean. "Henry seems very bright. What an amazing turnaround."

"Ja. He is a strong man. He has recovered well. It took quite a while for him to warm up this time. I think he will not be ill again, as long as we keep him warm," said Vulle.

A shooting star streaked across the sky above them, disappearing just above the horizon. The sound of snowmobiles in the distance drifted over the camp. The faint noises of reindeer grazing and grunting, close by in the dark, slipped between the cabins, with the clank of reindeer bells adding to the Christmas spirit.

"The young Dutch people are out exploring on the snowmobiles again," said Vulle, and he looked at Everton. "I hope they are not getting up to any mischief."

"If they're not careful, they might get caught by a troll," said Everton. "This is Troll Mountain, after all."

Vulle threw his head back and laughed.

"I don't know how they find their way around the countryside," said Jean. "It is so dark out there, and everything is covered in snow."

"You are right, Jean," said Vulle. "When we travel with the reindeer, sometimes with our families we have to remember every rock, every small hill, and every large tree so that we can find our way back to our lavvu. This is especially important if there is snow falling hard. It you can only see for ten paces, you have to rely on a list of landmarks in your head. These days snowmobiles, the new vehicles, and tracking devices make things easier, but people still become confused when the snow falls thickly. It is very easy to get lost," said Vulle.

"They are young, and they think they're immortal," said Jean.

"Christmas dinner will be ready by about three p.m. I will see you both then," said Vulle.

They had arrived at Everton and Jean's cabin. As Vulle walked off across the camp towards the large lavvu where he and his family were staying, the aurora exploded into the sky above them.

Lines of green, blue, and yellow rippled and danced, combined and separated, in bands stretching from horizon to horizon.

Jean and Everton stared at the spectacle.

"I think this is the fourth or fifth display of lights we have seen. Fantastic. Some people come here and never see the lights. We have been very fortunate. I don't think I would ever get tired of this," said Jean.

They entered their warm cabin, where they could take off most of their layers.

"What do you make of Henry's dramatic recovery?" said Everton. "Could it be that Sárá healed him? Did the spirits of wolves and ravens weave a magic spell on the Christian from America? Did she make any difference to his illness at all, or was she just reassuring us all while he recovered spontaneously?"

"Of course, the truth is we can't be sure," said Jean. "We don't know what would have happened if Sárá had done nothing. To be sure, we would need a control group of identical people who did nothing, and then we could compare outcomes. Actually, to be statistically significant, we would need tens or hundreds of patients, half doing nothing and half providing Sami shaman healing. However, it is certain that Henry was quite seriously ill. He spent almost all of the last twenty-four hours unresponsive, not eating or drinking. Remember, it was only yesterday evening that we were asking Vulle to call an evacuation helicopter. So Henry's apparent recovery is quite spectacular. He certainly had a good appetite when he woke. I just hope he remains well," said Jean.

Just before 3:00 p.m. the tourists started arriving at the dining cabin. A Christmas tree had been conjured up by the Issákson family. It was decorated with tiny glittering reindeer, trolls, elves, and Santa Clauses.

The guests sat at the wooden benches while Sárá and Oskár served drinks.

The last guests to arrive were Beth and Henry. As they entered the cabin, the talking subsided. The two Italian children hugged their parents. Rolf and Ulva looked at each other with raised eyebrows.

Rolf stood and turned to Vulle. "Surely it is not safe for the American to be here mixing with all of us while he is ill."

"Henry is better now. He has fully recovered. He is welcome to eat Christmas dinner with us. Please be reassured about this," said Vulle.

"This is not acceptable," said Rolf. "With respect, Vulle, you are not a doctor. We could all be a risk if we share the cabin with the American. I must insist that he is confined to his cabin on health grounds. He should really not be in the camp, let alone in the same cabin as us. You are risking the health of everyone else."

"I am just fine. Whatever was wrong with me has cleared," said Henry. "Beth and I will sit over here on our own. You don't need to worry about me. I won't come near you and your wife."

Henry started to walk to a bench set apart.

"Come and sit with us," said Everton. "Don't worry about Rolf. You are very welcome, and a merry Christmas to you."

"Ja, yes. Mr. Everton is right," said Vulle. "Henry and Beth are most welcome. There is no reason to worry. They are not infectious. Henry was ill, but now he is well. Come and join us, Henry."

Rolf's eyes blazed. He stood, pulled on his coat, and walked towards the door. "Come, Ulva. We will take our Christmas dinner alone. Away from this ridiculous *torrheit*. In future, we will be eating in our cabin, Vulle. When we get back to Germany, you will be hearing from my lawyers," said Rolf.

Ulva hastily put on her parka coat and followed Rolf.

"Don't worry, everyone. We will make sure that Rolf and Ulva get a good dinner. Now let's get started," said Vulle.

Vulle and his family had prepared a roast dinner with reindeer meat. For dessert, the tourists were served rice pudding. Hidden in the rice pudding was a single almond. The person who found the almond was to be given a marzipan pig as a prize. This was a great honour, of course. Sárá found the almond in her rice pudding, and the marzipan pig was soon devoured, although she gave the pig's head to Jean and the tail end of the pig to Oskár—sibling kindness of a special Sami type.

Henry and Beth both ate well. There were no signs of any lack of appetite.

After dinner, in the early evening, Christiaan and his two Dutch friends left early and once again took the snowmobiles out for a trip in the countryside. The buzz from their snowmobiles was disappearing into the distance. The Christmas dining cabin was lit by candles, which flickered gently. Shadows danced on the walls and ceiling. The central wood fire cast a warm orange glow around the cabin.

Jean and Everton lingered at their table, enjoying a Christmas shot of Bivrost gin and tonic.

Sárá was sitting quietly with her head buried in a book, oblivious to her surroundings. She appeared to be nearing the end of the book.

"What are you reading, Sárá?" said Jean.

Sárá turned the cover of her book to Jean. The embossed writing on the cover said *A Study in Scarlet*. "One of my Christmas presents. This is the first Sherlock Holmes novel that Sir Arthur Conan Doyle wrote," said Sárá. "I think it is perhaps one of his best. It describes a clash of two cultures and the harm that this can cause for normal people. Of course, Mr. Holmes solves the mystery with his superhuman powers of observation, logic, and deduction."

The candles cast a warm glow around the cabin. Shadows danced over the walls as the small group talked and drank.

"Have you read any books by Charles Dickens?" said Everton.

"I have, Mr. Everton. I enjoyed *A Tale of Two Cities*," said Sárá.

Sárá paused for a few seconds as if recalling something, then started again.

"Did you know that Mr. Dickens had many dogs and that his favourite dog was called Turk?" said Sárá. "We have some folktales about an evil ogre called a Dog-Turk. A Dog-Turk has the muzzle of a dog but otherwise is like a human being. As you might imagine, a Dog-Turk has much better smell sense than the average human.

"One day, long before Tromsø was a true city, a pair of Sami Christian girls lived there. A Russian ship arrived at the small town, and the Russians kidnapped the two girls, who were sisters. The only things they had with them were their clothes and their Bibles. The Russians sold the girls to a Dog-Turk, who immediately started to fatten them up to eat later. The Dog-Turk put each girl in her own pen for fattening up. Every day the Dog-Turk came and stabbed them with a fingernail to see if they were fat enough to eat. One of the girls ate all the food that the Dog-Turk gave her, but the other girl barely touched it.

"The Dog-Turk promised the devil, whom we call Baergalak, the girls in return for good luck. The girls knew about this promise and protected themselves from the evil one by keeping 'the books,' by which we mean the Psalms and the New Testament, with them at all times and by sleeping with the Bible under their heads. Each time the devil came to collect them, he said, 'Your father has given you to me,' but the girls answered, 'We have no other father than God in heaven.' So Baergalak had to go away empty handed.

"One day, when the Dog-Turk and his wife went out for some stealing and to inspect their tobacco fields, they told their servant to start a fire in the oven and roast one of the girls for their evening meal when they came home. The servant, who was an old woman, lit a fire in the oven. When the wood was reduced to burning coals, she asked the fat girl to rake out the coals, saying she was so old and feeble she could not manage to handle the long oven rake. The girl understood what was happening, jumped up, pushed the old woman into the glowing oven, roasted her, and prepared her for dinner for the two Dog-Turks. When this was done, she fetched her sister, and they hid in the cellar.

"When the Dog-Turks came home for their dinner, they soon saw what had happened and angrily began to search for the girls. They did not think to search the cellar. They ran straight to their tobacco fields and hunted there. As it became dark, they had not found the girls, so they returned home and went to sleep. The two girls crept from the cellar and dashed out into the tobacco fields, where there was such a strong smell of tobacco that the Dog-Turks had difficulty tracking anyone.

"In the morning, the Dog-Turk found the fat girl, bound a handkerchief round her eyes, and carried her out to the slaughtering place, where he murdered her. The thin girl had taken food with her and stayed in the field for a whole week. She escaped up a river, which erased her tracks. She reached a waterfall and hid herself in the empty space under the fall, inside a rock. After a week of searching, the Dog-Turk gave up and went home.

"The girl escaped over the river, where she met some people at war with each other. She asked both sides to help her and said whichever side helped her would win the battle. One side promised to help her, so they won the battle. They managed to get her on a ship that took her back to Tromsø.

"Back in Tromsø, the girl who escaped returned to her family of seven Christians. On the ship back to Tromsø, she had been pursued by some Russians, called Chudes, who wanted to kill her. The girl and her family found refuge in a cave and lay down to sleep. After they were asleep, a spider came along and wove a web across the cave's entrance. When the Russians walked past the cave, they saw the spun web and thought that nobody could have entered the cave recently. Eventually, they gave up their pursuit and lay down to sleep in another cave in Tromsø.

"The Christians slept for three hundred years before waking up. They left their cave and walked around Tromsø. The town had grown much larger than before. When they went to sleep, there was only one merchant. Now there were many. They could not recognise the town, and their money had grown so old that nobody would accept it.

"Then they understood they had slept for three hundred years. Later they went back to see what had become of their Russian pursuers. All that remained of them was a little dust.

"It is possible that my family and I are descended from that girl who survived the Dog-Turk, the devil, and the Russians, and who lived for three hundred years."

"I think you might be right about that," said Jean, draining her small glass of Bivrost.

As Jean and Everton walked back to their cabin, their stomachs were groaning with the arctic feast. They could hear the gentle rattle of reindeer bells surrounding the camp.

"Those Dutch youngsters are spending most of their time out on snowmobile rides," said Jean. "They don't seem very interested in the reindeer, or the dogs, or Sami culture, or even the aurora."

Outside the camp lights, in the forest surrounding the clearing, the lone wolf, which had been following them since Camp Arktis, sat watching and waiting.

CHAPTER 9

The Sacred Forest

THE NEXT MORNING, BOXING Day morning, Vulle came to Everton's cabin. Although it was morning, it remained as dark as midnight. Vulle's head torch shining through the windows announced his arrival outside the cabin door.

Jean and Everton were both enjoying a cup of tea. Vulle stamped the snow off his boots, removed his fur gloves and hat, and sat with them at the small table in their cabin.

"I have some news from Tromsø," said Vulle. "Not very good, I am afraid. The travel ban is still in force. They have again refused permission for Henry to visit the hospital in Tromsø or Oslo for a medical check, even though he remains well. They don't want any of us to leave Camp Trollfjell. It is ironic because this morning Henry is in great form. No signs of any illness. He is eating like a bear. The people in Tromsø are ordering that the entire camp should be quarantined for at least two weeks before any medical tests can be done on Henry in the Tromsø hospital. They say they might send in a medic if the roads are clear in a few weeks. The Christmas holiday period complicates the matter and slows down any testing, of course. It seems they have really locked us down. It is like the quarantine system for plague in the Middle Ages."

"Several weeks. We will have to stay here for several weeks. Rolf and his wife are not going to be happy when they hear this. Personally, I wouldn't mind a bit. I could get used to this lifestyle," said Everton.

"Yes. I suppose it is a bit better for us out here, rather than being in a city," said Vulle. "We are already isolated, but we have all the facilities, food, and supplies we need, and we have plenty of space and good transport for off-road travelling. We can move around hundreds of square kilometres of open country but still remain socially isolated from other people. In the cities, it would be worse being confined to houses or flats. Just because a handful of people in London and New York became ill at the same time. There have not been any more cases or deaths in the past couple of days. It seems like a hysterical reaction from medical and political bureaucrats to me. They are scared of one death in the middle of a big city, but if thousands die in the countryside because we cannot get access to health care, they don't give a…well, you know what I mean. Politicians are not my favourite species."

"I think we need to accept that our stay here is going to be quite a bit longer than we had planned," said Jean. "We must accept the inevitable and make the most of it. We will certainly learn a great deal from Sárá about Sami heritage from an extended visit."

"There are worse places to be stuck for weeks in the winter. It's dark here, but we keep seeing the aurora. That is worth a great deal. The wildlife is fantastic too, especially the spooky spirit wolves, which we never quite seem to see," said Everton.

"You'll have to teach us more about reindeer herding, and we can lend a hand while we are here, to make ourselves useful," said Jean.

Vulle smiled. "Well, there is not much work to do at present, of course. You are welcome to try working with the reindeer if you want to. It is physically very hard. We have a high risk of physical injury when we have to handle the animals. Large animals like reindeer are not always predictable. Even the domesticated reindeer. They are not humans. And they are much stronger than us. If they become worried, they can hurt us accidentally," he said.

"I've seen your little Sárá with the reindeer. And Oskár. They handle them expertly," said Everton.

"Ja. They are quite good," said Vulle, beaming with pride. "The reindeer can tell when they are confident and calm. Just like any other animal, I suppose."

"And your Sárá has a brilliant mind, Vulle. You must encourage her to put that brain to good use. For her age, she is streets ahead of most children. She has a great future ahead of her," said Jean.

"*Streets ahead*. That is interesting language. The English must measure brain power in streets. An unusual unit for intelligence," said Vulle. "How many streets of brain power does an average person have, I wonder. Was Mr. Einstein a twenty-street brain?"

"It is a figure of speech, Vulle. I think you know what I mean," said Jean.

"Yes. Sárá has always been a quick learner. She said her first word at the age of only three months. It was 'mamma,' of course. Daddy was out walking with reindeer," said Vulle. "But she is already planning her life out. She does not need me to encourage her. She will probably be a doctor, and perhaps the Norwegian minister of health, if she wants it, knowing her."

"Well, good for her. I am sure she will be brilliant, whatever she decides," said Jean.

There was a pause. It was the sort of pause that meant that Vulle was preparing to say something about which he was in two minds.

"I have been seeing some wolf tracks outside the cabins," said Vulle.

"Really? Any problems with the reindeer?" said Everton.

"No. Not so far. We don't usually have problems at this camp. Wolves, lynx, and wolverines stay away from the camp. They know humans are dangerous. Brown bears are hibernating at this time of year, of course. But I have seen wolf tracks among the cabins over the past two days. The dogs did not shout much, which is surprising. They normally smell bears or wolves and give us a good warning. This wolf doesn't seem to be interested in the reindeer. He is sniffing around the cabins."

"Do you think this puts us in danger? Should we be taking some extra precautions outside?" said Jean.

"I am not sure. It looks like just one wolf. A large one, with large paws. He seems to be wandering around the cabins, but nobody has actually seen him yet. The three young Dutch travellers have been enjoying the snowmobiles every day, out and about around the hills and forests. They have not reported seeing anything. I have not told the rest of the tourists staying with us. I don't want to make them more anxious, especially with Henry being ill and then the travel problems. We should probably keep this between us for now," said Vulle.

There was another pause. They all looked out of the triple-glazed window. The snow lay deep and smooth over the camp. The arctic darkness hid almost everything outside the lights of the camp. The lights reflected off occasional reindeer grazing around the camp. Some pauses in conversation are just pauses.

This variety was a statement that Vulle was about to announce the main reason for his morning visit.

"I have an idea. We might be able to get permission to travel a little sooner. We might be able to stop the quarantine of our camp. It is just possible. I wanted to ask you both what you think of it," said Vulle.

"OK. Tell us more," said Everton.

"I have a relative. She is Sami, and she works in the medical service at a nearby military base. Her name is Sofe. She is quite a senior medical and military officer," said Vulle.

"And?" said Everton.

"We are not supposed to have contact with people outside Camp Trollfjell, of course, because the politicians have decided to take us back to the Middle Ages. However, Sofe is based at the military base at Helligskogen. This is only about twenty kilometres away. We could get there and back in a day easily if the weather is good."

"So, what would we need Sofe to do for us? How could she help end the quarantine?" said Everton.

"Henry seems very well at present. Ánne has suggested something to me," said Vulle. "If we can ask Sofe to run some medical tests on Henry's blood, we might be able to exclude any serious infections. If we can exclude anything sensational like Ebola fever or the diseases that the people in London and New York suffered, this would enable us to tell the geniuses in Tromsø. If we do this, we might convince them that Henry never suffered any serious or contagious illness at all. This might mean that they allow you all to travel back to the city on time. I don't know about the international flights, but at least those who want to go to Tromsø or Oslo can."

"That sounds quite sensible and practical," said Jean. "What's the catch?"

"Well, technically we would be breaking the rules about quarantining everyone at Camp Trollfjell. Someone would need to travel to Helligskogen with a blood sample from Henry and pass it to Sofe for testing," said Vulle.

"Have you spoken to Sofe about this?" said Jean.

"Oh yes. I called her this morning. She is delighted to help. She has a mind of her own. She will happily run these tests for us, as long as I can get the sample to her. We can pass the sample to her in a way that ensures control of any infection. She is senior enough at Helligskogen that she can order tests. They have modern medical facilities there."

"And how would we get a blood sample from Henry?" said Everton.

"That's easy. We have some basic medical facilities on camp here. Ánne is a trained nurse. She has the equipment to take a blood sample and the skills. Cold storage is not a problem, of course. Nature is our friend for this. Once we have the sample, I suggest that I can take the dogs and travel to Helligskogen. We can be there and back within a day," said Vulle.

"Sounds like a good plan," said Jean. "Why did you want our opinion about it?"

Vulle looked back and forwards between Everton and Jean. "I was thinking that you might want to come with me, Everton."

"And why exactly does Kenneth have to go with you?" said Jean.

"For one thing, it is always safer to travel with two," said Vulle. "One person to go for help in the event of a problem. Actually, it is even safer to travel with three people."

"Mmm. This all sounds like an excuse for a boys' trip in the countryside to me," said Jean. "But it is a good idea. It might allow us all to get home on time, if it works. And it might stop Rolf and his wife bursting a blood vessel due to plague phobia. Why wouldn't Edo go with you?"

"Edo could come with me, but I would rather leave him here in case any of the other guests need to be…given any guidance. Either Edo or I should stay in the camp in case anything serious goes wrong," said Vulle.

"Well, I'm more than happy to accompany you to this place, Hell's Kogen, or whatever the name was," said Everton, smiling. "And we won't be gone more than a few hours, will we?"

"Probably not," said Vulle. "Depending on the weather, of course."

"OK. Let's do it," said Everton. "Let's go to Hell's Kitchen."

"Yes. The name is unusual. The name of the military camp is Helligskogen. This is a strange coincidence," said Vulle.

"In what way?" said Jean.

"Henry's dream. You remember he told us about his meeting with Grim, who told him to tell Sárá that she could find an answer in the Sacred Forest. Well, Helligskogen in English—it means the Sacred Forest," said Vulle.

CHAPTER 10

The Inhospitable Cabin

By midmorning on December 26, Vulle and Everton were ready to travel to Helligskogen.

Ánne had taken blood from Henry. Vulle had several small vials of blood, fully labelled and cushioned by Bubble Wrap, in a zipped-up pouch on the arm of his parka coat. Vulle and Everton harnessed eight dogs to one sled. They worked under the camp lights. The sky remained velvet black and clear of clouds. There was a bitingly cold wind. Despite this, the dogs were yapping excitedly, keen to get out on a run.

Everton watched Vulle carry a large sack filled with supplies and lash it to the sled.

"I thought we were planning to be back within a few hours?" said Everton, surprised that Vulle was bringing so much.

"We always need to be prepared for anything. The weather could break. Sometimes the unexpected happens. People and dogs are not perfect machines. We need to be flexible enough to cope with any delays for any reason," said Vulle.

Vulle took his rifle off his shoulder and secured it to the sled. He looked at Everton. "Just in case," he said.

Both Vulle and Everton were wearing their fox-fur hats. They looked like two brothers, one tall and one short. One slim and one sturdy. Vulle was clothed mostly in furs, even down to seal-skin boots. Everton's clothes were mostly layers of man-made garments.

Ánne, Oskár, Sárá, and Jean crunched across the deep snow, in the cold wind, to see them off.

"Good luck. Look after the Englishman," said Ánne, kissing Vulle on the cheek.

"And you behave yourself. Do exactly what Vulle tells you to," said Jean to Everton.

As they talked, Beth and Henry joined them. They linked arms, and Henry helped Beth to walk in the deep snow.

"Thanks a bunch for doing all this for me," said Henry. "I won't forget this."

The small group were being watched. From inside the warmth of his cabin, Rolf was standing at a window. His eyes narrowed as he looked at Henry and Beth. From farther out, in the darkness of the forest, outside the lights of the camp, a large wolf stood in the snow and watched. His bright blue eyes were fixed like a spotlight on the small form of Sárá. Small prey are easier to handle.

Everton sat on the sled. Vulle stood on the footboard, released the claw brake, and shouted for the dogs to run. They needed no encouragement and leaped into a run. The sled swished away from the camp, heading towards a well-worn forest track, east towards Helligskogen.

For several kilometres after they left the Trollfjell clearing, they passed through dense pine forest. The ground was gently undulating. The trees thinned out eventually, and they emerged into open countryside, which was covered in deep snow. They could see more patches of pine forest emerging from the snow ahead of them.

There was a half moon to light their way. Vulle kept his head torch on, and the dogs steered the sled expertly. They crossed several frozen streams and a river that was frozen into solid blue without incident.

Vulle kept the dogs running for two hours before stopping for a break and a meal. The dogs were fed with frozen meat. Vulle and Everton ate a packed meal prepared by Ánne, with some warm coffee from a thermos.

"This place, Helligskogen, where we are heading, used to be a military base during the Cold War," said Vulle. "At that time, our military kept tons of explosives under the bridges and on the roads in case of a Soviet invasion. The soldiers used to check the explosives three times every day. The Cold War had reached its icy hand north into the frozen Norwegian, Finnish, and Sami country. We were constantly ready to blow up everything to stop the Soviet invaders."

"Amazing to think back now to a time when we really thought that the Soviets might invade Western Europe. What a terrible waste of time and effort for millions of people. Seventy years without progress for the Russians," said Everton.

"Ja. But really it was only a short period of madness. Seventy years of communist delirium. For the Sami people, this is an instant of time only. We have experienced many similar periods of stagnation or worse from visiting cultures. We have been here for thousands of years. We have seen these borders and countries coming and going. Countries, kings, emperors, tyrants, and governments are temporary to us. We live our lives on a longer timescale. Most of the time we can ignore them all because the conditions in the north are too severe for them to occupy our land or to bother us. That is why we don't bother fighting back most of the time. Nature will do it for us," said Vulle.

Suitably fed, the dogs and the two men continued their journey. After another hour travelling across unsullied tundra covered in snow, they crossed a road that lay under several feet of snow. A line of poles marked the position of the road under the snow. Without the poles, there was no sign that the road existed. As they crested a small ridge, a group of buildings lay ahead of them, about a kilometre away. The lights of the buildings stood out in the permanent darkness of the arctic winter. A fence surrounded the buildings, with perimeter lights along the fence dotting the countryside. There was a well-lit entry gate in the fence, which was clearly the only way into or out of the military base.

Vulle encouraged the dogs towards the gate. They rapidly closed the distance. Vulle's head torch was lit. They could see some human activity at the gate. It was clear that the soldiers at the gate post were aware of their approach.

Vulle stopped the sled a hundred metres from the gate post. "Let me take your warrant card to show them," he said.

Everton unzipped a pouch in his parka coat, fished out his UK police warrant card, and handed it to Vulle.

Two soldiers dressed in warm, white arctic clothing walked out to meet Vulle. They both held weapons, which were pointed at the ground. Vulle held up his hands and shouted a greeting in Norwegian. The soldiers shouted back. They stopped ten metres apart. Vulle turned, pointed to Everton on the sled, and said something in Norwegian. Everton stood and waved to the soldiers. A brief conversation in Norwegian took place between Vulle and the soldiers. At one point, Vulle took out something and placed it on the snow in front of him, together with Everton's warrant card, before moving back a few steps. The soldiers advanced with a torch and inspected the object on the ground, then said something briefly to Vulle and walked back to their gate post.

Vulle stepped forwards again, picked up the object on the snow, and walked back to Everton. He handed Everton the warrant card.

"I have explained who I am, and I showed them our ID. I have asked them to talk to Major Sofe Issaksdatter and told them she is expecting us. They seem quite nervous. They have been ordered not to have any contact with any civilians due to the international travel restrictions. I think they are contacting Sofe. We will see," said Vulle. "It should not take too long either way."

The wind was rising, and it had started to snow lightly. The dogs were curled up on the snow. They seemed to have detected that the humans had decided to stop running in the snow for a while. They settled in for a period of boredom while the humans talked to each other as usual.

Several minutes elapsed, and then, from within the military compound, a military vehicle drove up to the gate post, headlights blazing. A small person emerged from the vehicle in the regulation white winter military uniform. A soldier at the gatepost emerged and saluted this new arrival. There was a short conversation between the soldiers, then the short soldier walked out to meet Vulle. It was now snowing more heavily. The gatepost was now only just visible to Vulle and Everton from a hundred metres.

Vulle turned to Everton. "This is Sofe. She will collect the blood sample, and then we must leave," he said.

Major Sofe approached to three paces and then stopped. She was hardly more than five feet tall. Under her white parka hood,

Everton could see short white-blond hair and the glacier-blue eyes typical of her family. Vulle raised his hand and said something in Sami. Sofe replied and pointed to the snow in front of him. Vulle took out the small bag containing the blood samples and placed it on the virgin snow at his feet. He beckoned to Everton, and they both retreated five paces. Sofe took out a clear plastic bag, walked up to the blood samples, reversed the bag around her gloves, picked up the blood samples, folded her bag around the samples, and sealed it. She placed the first bag on snow, took out another clear plastic bag, reversed this, picked up her first bag with the second bag as a glove, and sealed the second bag.

Sofe looked up and raised a hand to Vulle and Everton. She said something in Sami, then added in English, directed towards Everton, "I should have your results in a few hours. I will let you know as soon as I have them."

She turned and walked back towards the gatepost. As she entered the military compound, the sentry soldiers saluted her again.

The snow was now falling heavily. Vulle and Everton could only just see the outline of the gatepost. They turned and retraced their steps back to the dogs and the sled. As they arrived, the dogs jumped up and started barking for another run. They knew when the humans had stopped nattering.

Vulle expertly turned the sled around, and the dogs sped off, back in the direction from which they had arrived. Everton could hardly see the tracks from their arrival, which were rapidly filling with snow. Despite this, Vulle and the dogs seemed confident of the direction of travel.

After several kilometres, they entered a forested area, travelling rapidly along a clear track between the trees. Everton did not recognise this part of the country from their journey out. The heavy snowfall was making it very difficult to recognise anything.

Two or three kilometres into the forest, they reached a small wooden cabin. There was no real clearing in the forest. The trees hugged close to the cabin, which lay directly next to the forest track. Vulle called the dogs to a halt and fixed the claw brake.

"This is where we will take a break," said Vulle. "The weather is closing in. Too difficult to travel in any case. Let's get warmed up inside and see what we find."

The snow around the cabin door was not deep. Someone had clearly used the cabin relatively recently. The door easily opened. Within a couple of minutes, Vulle had unloaded the sled into the cabin and started a fire in the wood-burning stove. He lit a couple of candles and then fed the dogs with frozen meat, thawed in bowls with boiled water. He and Everton started to warm up in the cabin and take stock of their situation.

"We should have the results from Sofe by tomorrow," said Vulle, placing his satellite phone on a rickety wooden table in the cabin. "Once the snow eases, we can travel back to Camp Trollfjell to let everyone know how things stand."

"Excellent. Everything seems to be going to plan," said Everton. "I am certainly glad I'm with you out here, Vulle. Without an expert guide, I would soon be completely lost in this wilderness. I can see how people die very easily in this arctic land."

Vulle prepared a simple meal and some hot tea from their supplies. It was midafternoon but still dark outside. The candles cast a flickering light around the cabin. As the meal was warming, the two men looked around the cabin. Against one wall, the candlelight flickered over a large number of clean and neatly stacked boxes with no dust covering them. Someone had visited this cabin recently and deposited these boxes for some reason. As they sat sipping their hot tea, Vulle gave Everton some historical perspective on their location.

"There is a fable about this cabin. It is called the inhospitable cabin by some of my countrymen," said Vulle. "The story goes something like this, if I can remember it. There were two reindeer herders moving their reindeer herd in the month of November in this area. This was a long time ago. It was clear and bitingly cold at that time. During their work, they had to cross an icy river, five or six metres wide. While walking across the ice, the lead reindeer herder fell through a patch of thin ice into the cold water. He was well dressed, with warm leather clothes, but he quickly became soaked. He began to freeze and tremble, and his clothes started to harden from the cold. He knew he would die if he did not find shelter quickly. The men knew of only one cabin within miles, but they were reluctant to go there. Among the migrant Sami, it was said that there was no peace to be had at that cabin, but they had no choice. So they made haste to get there.

"When they arrived, they lit a fire. The wet man took off his clothes and hung them up to dry. Then he lay on the cabin floor. It was dark, as it is now, and the only fire was from the open door of the wood-burning stove. As they warmed up, the wet man and his companion started to snooze. They lay there half asleep and half awake. After a while, the wet man woke to hear someone approaching the cabin. He thought this was strange but assumed it was one of his brothers who also herded reindeer in this area. The sound of footprints grew louder and louder. The sound of the footprints had much longer steps than his brother. There was a long gap between each step as it hit the snow. This was worrying. The man sat up and thought about the legend that there was no peace to be had in the cabin.

"Suddenly the man heard the front door open. The door opened slowly. A leather-clad person tried to enter the cabin. But not the whole person. The new visitor was so large that only his lower body, from the waist down, could fit into the cabin. The herder could not see the upper body of the new visitor. Only the legs could be seen in the cabin.

"The herder was terrified. This huge stranger was so big that he could not fit in a cabin. What sort of creature could this be? The herder was certain that he was doomed. He expected a troll to tear off the roof of the cabin and to dash out his brains at any second. He lay on the cabin floor and waited to die.

"But he did not die. Slowly, the visitor withdrew his legs. Instead of killing the herders, the mysterious stranger pulled his legs out of the cabin. There was a pause, without any sound. The herders waited for the monster to smash the roof. Instead, they listened as the footsteps gradually disappeared into the forest again. They had been lucky to escape with their lives.

"As soon as the clothes were dry, the reindeer herder and his companion quickly dressed and left the cabin. They never returned. The tall, leather-clad creature that had tried to get into their cabin was never seen by anyone else. Since that time, nobody who has visited the cabin has ever slept well there."

Vulle smiled at Everton and sipped his hot drink.

"I am guessing that this is the very cabin in which the herders were almost victims of a hungry troll," said Everton, smiling at Vulle.

Vulle nodded. "You are right about this, Everton. We are sitting in the haunted cabin. I hope you are not superstitious."

"Now, that is interesting, Vulle," said Everton. "You and your family have been telling us tales of supernatural spirits throughout our journey with you. Wolf spirits. Reindeer maidens. Fox ghosts. And now you tell me not to be superstitious. You are a joker."

Vulle chuckled and stared at the red glow from the wood stove. "It's up to you what you believe, Everton. I am just telling you some tales to pass the time."

"So, what was this creature that nearly killed the herders? What do you think it was?" said Everton.

"Nobody knows," said Vulle. "It might have been a troll. The two herders were lucky that it didn't dash their brains out and eat them both."

"It might also have been a dream. They might both have been exhausted and asleep, with minds full of Sami legends," said Everton.

"Yes, but I think they both had the same dream. Surely that is impossible. And a dream would not be as interesting as a close encounter with a troll," said Vulle.

"It certainly is a great story to tell a guest visiting this cabin for the first time," said Everton, smiling at Vulle. "You know how to ensure that your guest sleeps soundly. If I here even the slightest sound overnight, I am going to have kittens."

"Kittens?" said Vulle. "This is not familiar to me. Having kittens is something that the English do when they are scared?"

"Yes. Essentially, that's right. The English have some strange habits, I agree. Now, what are we going to do about these boxes?" said Everton.

The two men talked over their options and took a closer look at the boxes.

Eventually, Vulle looked out the single small cabin window. "This snow is still falling heavily," he said. "We call this type of snow *giel*. We may have to stay here overnight. This should not be a problem. As soon as the snow eases, we can start back to Camp Trollfjell."

CHAPTER 11

Flyover

IN CAMP TROLLFJELL, WHILE Vulle and Everton were travelling to the Sacred Forest for their meeting with Sofe, Jean spent most of the time with Sárá.

Jean put on her multiple layers and walked out to meet the reindeer with Sárá. Many of the reindeer were quite content for Jean and Sárá to walk up to them and even stroke them. Most of the reindeer simply ignored the humans. They were far more concerned with pushing the snow aside with their hooves and eating the lichen or moss growing on the ground underneath the snow.

Oskár and Edo were looking over the reindeer herd, wearing head torches in the arctic darkness to pick out any weak or injured animals. The reindeer seemed to accept the humans wandering among them. The clank of reindeer bells and the grunts of the animals as they grazed were soothing sounds in the otherwise silent, snow-covered countryside.

Jean and Sárá watched as Oskár and Edo skilfully caught reindeer while avoiding the sharp horns.

"The horns can cause serious eye injuries," said Sárá. "The reindeer have been herded into this corral. Edo and Oskár are checking the teeth of some of the older reindeer to ensure they will make it through the winter and survive another year. Those with old and worn teeth are being separated from the herd. We will kill these reindeer and use their meat, skin, and antlers. In fact, we use everything from the reindeer."

"Teeth are very important," said Jean. "For humans, bad teeth used to mean a death sentence too before modern dentistry and antibiotics. Many skeletons we find from antiquity show dental abscesses as the final illness before death."

"Yes, our Sami healing is not so good for a dental abscess," said Sárá. "If I had a serious dental infection, I would see a modern dentist and take modern antibiotics. There is a limit to the power of our Sami spirits."

Sárá smiled at Jean as if she were confiding a secret. Jean smiled back and nodded in full agreement.

As they watched the reindeer, it started to snow. Within minutes, the snow was falling heavily. Jean and Sárá walked back to the cabins. As they walked between pine trees on the edge of the camp clearing, Sárá stopped and turned to her left to stare into the forest. Jean looked in the direction Sárá was staring. In the dark recesses of the forest, between the pine trunks, her head torch briefly picked out the reflection of two red eyes staring back.

"Did you see that?" said Jean. "There is something watching us."

"Mmm. You are right," said Sárá. "It has been watching for a while. It followed us up to the corral and back again."

"What is it?" said Jean.

"I am not sure. A wolf, I think. But it is alone, which is unusual. It seems interested in us. Jean, what do you think about the Sami stories of spirits? Animals that can take human form and humans that can walk with animals. Do you think the Sami people are crazy?"

Jean thought for a few seconds before responding. "I don't think Sami beliefs are crazy, Sárá. I think your beliefs are in context with the times when they were formed, thousands of years ago for some of them. Many beliefs in England were similar before we knew about the laws of physics, biology, chemistry. People in England in the Middle Ages also believed in animal spirits, witches, demons, and evil spirits."

"Do you read Harry Potter stories?" said Sárá.

"Actually, yes. I really like all the Potter books," said Jean.

"I have all the stories about Harry Potter," said Sárá. "I have read them all many times. I particularly love Snape, and Dobby. Of course, I know they don't really exist. But while I read the books, my mind suspends reality, and I inhabit a mental world in which I see them and feel for them. I am sad when they are sad. I know that the magic of Harry Potter, Severus Snape, and Dobby cannot happen in my universe, but my mind allows it to happen in the imaginary universe. Perhaps the Sami beliefs are a bit like beliefs in the magic of Snape and He Who Must Not Be Named? It is real in their world."

"You might be right," said Jean. "There are also parts of the story of Harry Potter that are very real in his world and in ours. The parts about the loss of his parents leaving a terrible, lifelong scar in his life. That is a real thing in our world, and sadly very common. Paul McCartney and John Lennon both lost parents at a young age, and I think this had a big impression on their lives."

"I don't know these two people, Paul and John," said Sárá. "But I understand what you mean. What did Paul and John do with their lives?"

Jean laughed. "They were musicians. That is, John was a musician, and Paul is still a musician. John died some time ago.

To answer your question about Sami beliefs more accurately, I think some of your beliefs are very helpful for your survival in this climate. They might not be exactly correct in terms of the scientific laws of nature, but if you follow them, you will probably survive and be safer. The belief in choosing very carefully the reindeer to be culled is one example. This is practical animal husbandry, as done by the Sami. And the tales about wolf spirits are very useful to keep your children alert to the dangers of large predators, of course."

"So, what would it take to convince you that a wolf was more than a wolf, or to convince you that a human could actually become a wolf?" said Sárá.

"I don't know for sure," said Jean. "I guess I will know when I see it."

Several hours later everyone in camp collected in the dining cabin. Rolf and his wife had relented and agreed to eat with the others, but they sat at a separate table.

Henry and Beth sat with Jean, Sárá, Edo, and Oskár. Vulle and Everton had not yet returned.

Edo and Oskár were talking in Sami. Jean picked up the word *Christiaan* as they spoke. The three Dutch tourists had not yet joined them for dinner.

"Daddy and Mr. Everton will have stopped somewhere safe as soon as the snow started to fall like this," said Sárá. "They might even be staying with Sofe in Helligskogen. They will probably stay there overnight. Once the snow stops, they will come back."

"I'm sure you're right," said Jean. "Knowing Kenneth, he will be having a great time. But where have the Dutch tourists got to, I wonder," said Jean.

Edo and Oskár looked at each other. Then Edo turned to Jean. "They took three snowmobiles this afternoon," he said. "We haven't seen them since then. They have been away for about four hours. We were expecting them back for dinner."

"Is there anything we can do to find them?" said Jean.

"It is difficult," said Edo. "These Dutch were very keen to explore on the snowmobiles alone. Without anyone to guide them. They were very confident of their ability. We tried to tell them that there were risks and that it is hard to find your way in our country, especially when it snows heavily like this. But they knew better than us, of course. Now we see the result. They are missing for a few hours, and there is little we can do to help them."

"Perhaps we can ask for a search-and-rescue helicopter if they don't make it back before the morning?" said Beth.

"Yes. We can ask for this," said Edo. "But with the current restrictions on travel, I am not sure how successful this would be. And if they are stuck in the snow for many hours, they may not survive."

As Edo spoke, there was a faint drumming sound from outside. Everyone stopped speaking and listened intently. The drumming sound was getting louder.

"That might be the snowmobiles?" said Beth.

"No, honey. I don't think so," said Henry. "That's the sound of a helicopter. Or perhaps several helicopters?"

The sound was now quite loud. Henry moved to one of the windows and looked out. Beth joined him. Rolf walked to another window, as far from Henry as possible.

It was still dark and snowing heavily. As the sound grew louder, it was possible to make out several lights passing overhead. At least three helicopters flew across the clearing. The regular thump of the rotating blades was deafening, despite the falling snow. They must have only been a few tens of metres above the ground. They flew over the camp and disappeared off towards the east. The sound rapidly diminished to nothing. There was silence in the cabin.

"It is very unusual for helicopters to fly in such heavy snow," said Edo. "There must be something important going on."

"Where would so many helicopters come from? We are many miles from the nearest city," said Henry.

"The only place with helicopters close to us would be the military base at Helligskogen," said Edo.

"That's where Vulle and Everton were heading," said Henry.

As they drifted back to their dinner tables, Rolf remained at the window, looking out into the falling snow. He turned to face the others. "Since Vulle is no longer with us, I suggest that we should choose someone else to take important decisions we face."

There was silence in the room.

Rolf continued, since nobody else spoke. "We have been cut off from civilization for several days. Now we see that there appears to be some form of military action taking place. We need some hierarchy in order to take decisions about how we reconnect with civilization and travel back to our countries. I propose that the adults among us elect a new leader right now and start taking the steps to get back to normal."

"I don't think your assessment is quite accurate, Rolf," said Ánne. "The temporary travel restrictions have been imposed on us. We are in touch with the authorities in Tromsø and Oslo by satellite phone. As soon as we are permitted, normal travel will resume."

"And what gives you the authority to decide these matters?" said Rolf.

"This is our property, our land, and our country," said Ánne, standing to face Rolf. "You are here as our guests. My family and I have the responsibility to ensure your safety while you are here. We have the skills and knowledge to keep you safe. The roads are not passable at present, even if you wished to leave. Nothing has happened that would make it appropriate for you to take over and start making decisions about leaving the camp."

"I think you are wrong about this, Mrs. Issákson," said Rolf. "Your husband and Mr. Everton have not returned. Three of our fellow travellers are missing. It seems to me that things are going badly wrong. You don't seem to be in control of events. I suggest we choose a change of priorities among ourselves. We need some decisive leadership."

It was Edo's turn to stand and speak. "You are free to leave at any time, Mr. Rolf," said Edo. "Nobody is stopping you. However, you have no dogs, no sleds, and no snowmobiles. These are owned by somebody else. How do you expect to walk over fifty kilometres back to Tromsø, across the mountains, through deep snow, in blizzards, in the arctic winter darkness? We are offering you a comfortable and safe place to stay until the travel situation returns to normal. We are not keeping you imprisoned here."

"What you say sounds so reasonable," said Rolf. "But the reality is that these decisions about staying here have been imposed upon us. When we originally paid you for an arctic safari, the arrangement was for a holiday for us to enjoy the northern lights and the culture of the Sami people. I did not sign up for imprisonment in an arctic concentration camp. I believe that we should return to Camp Arktis as soon as possible and then drive back to Tromsø in preparation for our journeys back to our home countries. I do not believe that the authorities in Tromsø would prevent us from entering the city. The German government would not permit this. If Henry and his wife wish to remain here, since they are the cause of our isolation, then of course this is up to them."

Sárá could contain herself no longer. She stood and walked towards Rolf. "You have no right to speak like this," she said. "You speak as if my daddy is not returning. I can assure you that he will be back with us shortly after the snow stops falling, with Mr. Everton. You speak about Henry as if he chose to be ill. You have no humanity when you talk like this. Henry is now much better, and he has no responsibility for the decision that we should stay here until the travel situation returns to normal. Without our help and support, you and your wife would not last two hours in our country. You have no right to try to pretend you are some sort of authority to take over our camp or that you have the power to make decisions here."

Sárá was standing only six feet from Rolf. Her arms were at her sides, shaking slightly, but her eyes were wide open and fixed on Rolf.

"Pah. Little children. Why are we listening to little children?" said Rolf, turning to the rest of the room.

"You are not showing any form of leadership by disrespecting others," said Ánne, moving to stand next to her daughter. "Sárá is speaking the truth. Vulle is very experienced travelling in these conditions. There are many safe places he can stay during difficult weather. He will be back very soon. If he had been in any difficulty, he would have called us with his satellite phone. You are making a serious mistake to assume that Vulle will not return."

"I simply don't believe you," said Rolf. "You and your daughter are hoping that Vulle will return, but you cannot guarantee this. Let's end this charade and take some clear decisions before things get worse."

As Rolf spoke, the sound of a snowmobile could be heard. It was faint at first but getting louder. The sound swiftly approached the dining cabin, then cut out just outside the cabin door. Footsteps could be heard moving towards the cabin door. Everyone looked towards the door, which swung open.

In the doorway stood Christiaan, the Dutch tourist. His parka coat was covered in newly fallen snow. He was holding a rifle in his hands, pointing it at the centre of the room.

Chapter 12

Christiaan

CHRISTIAAN STOOD IN THE doorway for a few seconds, taking in the scene before him. Snow billowed in through the open door behind him. He was slightly breathless. He looked around the room, trying to judge what was happening, then turned towards Edo.

"I need some supplies, and I need the snowmobile to be filled with petrol. I will be taking it and leaving. I need these things immediately. No delays. Please, would you get these things for me at once?" he said, waving his rifle towards Edo.

Edo looked at Ánne, uncertain how to react. Ánne looked at Christiaan holding his rifle, then nodded to Edo. Edo started to walk towards the door.

"The rest of you all need to stay in this cabin. None of you will be harmed, as long as you stay calm and do as I tell you," said Christiaan.

Rolf was the person closest to Christiaan. Rolf stepped forwards. Despite being more than forty years older than Christiaan and almost a foot shorter, he was not hesitant. "I don't know what you are trying to do, young man, but you will not succeed. We will not be intimidated by you waving a rifle in our faces," said Rolf.

Christiaan did not hesitate either. He reversed the rifle and struck Rolf hard in the face with the rifle butt. Rolf collapsed to the floor, emitting a short grunt as he fell. He lay still, groaning. Blood spurted from his nose and upper lip. It was unlikely that Rolf would be able to speak for some time. Christiaan smiled and raised the rifle again in preparation to hit Rolf on the floor.

"No!" shouted Sárá, who stood closest to Rolf. She darted forwards and placed herself between Rolf and the rifle butt. She held up both her hands. "He is not able to defend himself," she said in a firm voice. Her hands shook slightly, but her tone was even. "You must not make things worse. Go. Take your snowmobile and supplies and leave us. Edo, help this man get out of here." This was a command, not a request.

Christiaan seemed to be convinced. He slowly lowered his rifle. "OK. Edo, come with me. We need to sort out the snowmobile quickly," he said. "And I will be taking this young lady with me."

Christiaan grabbed Sárá's outstretched hand. He pulled her with him as he walked towards the door. "And if any of you leave this cabin, the tiny Sárá won't be so chatty anymore," he said.

Edo walked out of the cabin, and Christiaan followed, pulling Sárá by the arm.

As soon as Christiaan had left the cabin, Ánne and Jean both ran to Rolf and helped him sit on a seat. He was breathing, moaning, and touching his face. His eyes were half closed, and he seemed unaware of his surroundings.

Oskár and the Italian family looked out the windows and watched Christiaan take Sárá and Edo to her lavvu. They soon emerged with Sárá clothed in her full travelling furs and fur hat. It was clear that Christiaan planned for Sárá to keep him company wherever he was going. From there, they crossed to the snowmobile storage hut. They could see Edo preparing a snowmobile.

Snow had finally stopped falling, but a dense mist was now drifting through the camp. The lights of the buildings only penetrated the mist for about ten metres, beyond which the dark arctic winter closed down all visibility.

After about ten minutes, Christiaan returned to the dining cabin, pushing Edo with his rifle barrel and pulling Sárá by her furry arm.

"Time for a meal and drink, I think," said Christiaan, nodding to Ánne. "Something fast and hot, please. Edo, you join the others."

He placed his rifle on the table nearest to the door and pulled Sárá to sit next to him.

Ánne stared at Sárá but was unable to speak. A tear ran down one of her cheeks.

"I am fine, Mum. Better get him some hot food before he beats up another old man," said Sárá, shaking the arm that Christiaan held.

"Cheeky," said Christiaan, and he let go of the arm just long enough to slap the back of Sárá's head hard once.

Sárá winced but said nothing and glared at Christiaan.

Ánne rushed to the kitchen. Within a few minutes, she came back with a hot stew, bread, and hot tea. Christiaan wolfed the food down, with Sárá standing silently beside him.

As he ate, the faint sound of dogs barking drifted into the cabin. Sárá heard it first. She turned to look out the windows and nodded as if she had been expecting this. Oskár also heard it and looked to Sárá for signs of what he should do. The Italians were huddled in a group, the children crying and talking in Italian whispers to their parents. Beth and Henry held hands but sat still.

Ánne and Christiaan heard the faint sound of dogs barking at the same time. Ánne stepped forwards without thinking.

Christiaan threw down his spoon, grabbed the rifle in one hand, and pulled Sárá up by her arm. "Don't," he shouted at Ánne. "Everyone stay exactly where they are. Nobody move a muscle. Now, Sárá and I are going on a short journey. I don't want to see any of you come through this door. If I do, Sárá will be a little more holy than she is now."

He backed out the door, pulling Sárá with him. The door swung shut behind them.

Jean, Oskár, and Ánne ran to the door and looked out into the dark arctic afternoon. The mist was drifting between cabins, obscuring their view intermittently.

Sárá and Christiaan disappeared into the mist. Seconds later the sound of a snowmobile firing up drifted across the camp. The sound of the snowmobile slowly faded into the distance.

CHAPTER 13

The Hunt

VULLE AND EVERTON MADE good time once the snow stopped falling. They followed the snowstorm as it receded to the west. It took less than two hours for the dogs to pull them from the inhospitable cabin back to Camp Trollfjell. During the second half of the journey, mist replaced the snow, cutting visibility down to less than twenty metres despite their head torches.

Ignoring the mist, the dogs were confident that they were heading home and pulled the sled with unerring accuracy to the camp.

The sled stopped outside the snowmobile shed, where the camp lights kept the arctic darkness at bay. Vulle stepped on the claw brake, stepped off the sled, and walked towards the dogs, which jumped and yapped with joy. They were expecting a good feed to reward their hours of running.

Just before Vulle unharnessed the first dog, Edo came running out of the mist, closely followed by Ánne and Jean.

Edo clasped Vulle's shoulders and spoke rapidly in Sami. Ánne interrupted intermittently, wringing her hands and pointing into the mist. Everton watched this unfold. The only words he understood were "Christiaan" and "Sárá." Everton looked at Jean with raised eyebrows.

"Christiaan has just taken Sárá as hostage," said Jean. "He took a snowmobile and left only a few minutes ago. He has a rifle. We don't know where the other Dutch people are. We don't even know why Christiaan is behaving like this. Some helicopters flew over the camp a short time ago. Probably military. What's been going on out there in the mist and snow?"

Everton looked at Vulle. Without speaking to each other, the two men knew that they had to leave immediately to chase down Christiaan and his little hostage. The dogs would have to wait for their meal.

Vulle spoke for a couple of minutes to Ánne in Sami. He spoke quietly, but there was a core of hard steel in his tone as he spoke. She simply nodded in response, bit her lip, and put both hands over her mouth.

"We go right now to get Sárá and to stop Christiaan," said Vulle, to Everton.

Everton did not need to reply. He simply nodded once.

Vulle slipped his rifle case off the sled and looped it over his head for quicker access. Everton sat on the sled again. The snowmobile had left clear tracks. A cry from Vulle, and the dogs jumped back into life. As they started to run, a couple of dogs looked back towards Vulle, as if to ask, "What about lunch, boss?" But their joy in running quickly took over. They all pulled hard, and the sled sped off, following the snowmobile tracks.

As Vulle and Everton left the lights of the camp, the arctic darkness and mist closed around them. The dogs stopped barking and concentrated on their task. They seemed to know that this run was for a serious purpose and not for pleasure.

Vulle concentrated on the fresh tracks ahead of the sled, which he could only see for around ten metres due to the mist.

The tracks were running due west, back towards the mountains that they had crossed when travelling from Camp Arktis.

Fifty metres from the sled, on their left side, a large wolf loped gently through the snow. He paralleled Vulle's sled perfectly, even though visibility was severely limited in the mist. His tireless gait suggested he could have run like this for days or weeks without rest. Indeed, he could have run indefinitely if necessary. His kind had almost limitless stamina. He made almost no noise, his large paws spreading and acting like snowshoes.

Vulle's sled entered the forest track, passing through the forest surrounding Camp Trollfjell. The wolf kept pace with the sled easily and silently, passing among the dark trunks of the pine trees.

The dogs knew that they had a fellow traveller. The lead dog, Čammo, looked to his left towards their companion animal. Mist obscured the wolf, but Čammo could tell he was there and the speed he was running. Čammo could also tell with his nose that the wolf was a friend and not an enemy in the current chase. So Čammo accepted the presence of a large predator so close to their sled and their humans, and the other dogs followed his lead.

As they slid across the snow, Everton noticed that the tracks of the snowmobile were sometimes stained with small areas of slightly bluish-green liquid. At first, this was only small spots, but as the kilometres passed, the stains seemed to appear more often.

Everton turned to speak to Vulle. "It looks like the snowmobile is leaking something," said Everton.

Vulle looked down at Everton, smiled, and nodded. "Edo made sure that the range of the snowmobile was limited before Christiaan left. He is losing fuel as he travels," Vulle said. "He will not reach Camp Arktis."

The ground started to rise under them, and the trees thinned out as they rose. Soon they were travelling in open country and rising towards the mountain pass, through which they had travelled on their journey out. As they rose, the mist slowly cleared. They emerged into an inky-black arctic afternoon, with a clear sky above them. The moon was not yet in the sky. The faint light of the stars, reflecting from the snow, provided just enough light to see the outline of the mountains on either side of the valley they were ascending.

As they emerged from the mist, the wolf that accompanied them fell back and moved off to the north several hundred metres. From this distance, he easily kept pace with the sled, but he also kept just outside the range of most human eyes. His large blue eyes could see much farther than the humans. He could see exactly where the motorised vehicle was up ahead, even though it was enshrouded in mist. He could smell the strange fluid that was leaking from the machine, and he knew this meant that their chase would be successful. He relished the hunt that they were making this night. He felt confident that his master would be pleased with the outcome of this hunt. He had made many kills during his long life. His current prey was not a difficult animal to hunt. The little girl was unusual. He did not fully understand why his master wanted to protect the girl, but he accepted that she was a great hunter and an important member of his pack whom he must keep safe.

Once or twice, Everton thought he might have heard a faint echo of a motor ahead of them. But this quickly dissipated, and he could see no sign of the snowmobile ahead of them.

They had been travelling for an hour when they reached the head of the mountain pass. They crested the rise and were able to see down the next valley towards the forest below and the frozen lake beyond that. The air was clear at the higher altitude of the mountain pass, but they could see that the mist lay thick over the lower reaches of the mountain, where the forest started, and on the flat plain of the frozen lake, which spread out below them.

The cold was intense. Everton's fingers and toes were hurting despite his double gloves, socks, thick boots, and the heavy rug over his legs. Both Vulle and Everton had face protectors covering their mouths and noses. Vulle's woollen cape covered his fur coat. He showed no signs of suffering with the cold or even being aware of it. He shouted to the dogs, who knew from his tone that they were not likely to get their food or any rest for some time to come.

As they started on the downhill course, Everton noticed that the leaking gasoline was becoming more pronounced. Clearly Edo had done a good job. *Perhaps a screwdriver through the petrol tank, or perhaps a loosened fuel pipe,* thought Everton. *Good for you, Edo. Well done.*

Vulle leaned forwards to speak into Everton's ear. "When we catch them, we should separate and move away from the dogs to protect our transport back and to give him multiple targets."

Everton nodded. The climax of their journey was approaching.

The sled entered the forest area as they descended. They started to pass through thin strands of mist. They could clearly hear the sound of the snowmobile ahead of them now. The mist gradually thickened as they descended. After a kilometre, the forest thinned out. The mist was now thick around them. The ground suddenly levelled out. They had reached the frozen lake. A thin layer of snow lay on top of the lake ice, which glowed blue in the lights of their head torches.

The sound of the snowmobile was now intermittent. It sounded as if it was having some difficulty. As they sped out onto the lake, following the tracks, the motor suddenly died. The only sound left was the faint swish of their sled on the lake ice.

Chapter 14

Freki

THE DOGS FOLLOWED THE snowmobile tracks. Vulle, Everton, and the wolf knew that their adversary was close. Mist obscured everything more than ten paces distant.

Suddenly, they emerged near to the stationary snowmobile.

Christiaan was standing next to it. He held his rifle in his right hand pointing horizontally at the new arrivals. In his left hand he held the hair at the back of Sárá's head tightly. Sárá was wincing with pain as he twisted her hair, but she made no sound. A few paces behind Christiaan, Everton and Vulle could see the dark patch of dark ice, which they had noticed the last time they crossed the frozen lake.

As soon as he saw the stationary snowmobile emerging from the mist, Vulle jumped on the claw brake, bringing the sled to a rapid halt. The dogs stopped running and looked around at their owner. They were not used to stopping on ice, even when it was covered with a dusting of snow.

As the sled skidded to a halt, Everton threw himself to his left and scrambled across the ice before standing to face Christiaan. Vulle calmly stepped off his sled bars and walked in the opposite direction, five paces to his right. His eyes never left the rifle in Christiaan's hand. Vulle's rifle case was still looped around his chest. The rifle was safely inside the case, utterly useless to Vulle in this contest.

Christiaan smiled as he faced his two adversaries. "Thank you for coming so quickly, Vulle," he said. "You arrived just in time. Little Sárá and I can now resume our journey with the loan of your excellent sled and dogs."

"Don't be stupid, Christiaan," said Everton. "The Norwegian military know where we are. Their helicopters will be here within the hour. You have no chance of escaping. Just put the rifle down, let Sárá go, and nobody will be harmed. You will just make matters worse for yourself if you harm the girl."

"You are mistaken, Mr. Everton," said Christiaan. "I have every chance of escaping. I have more friends than you can guess in powerful places in this country. If I see any sign of the helicopters that you mention, I promise you that Sárá will never see another sunrise or another spring. I am sure that you will tell your military friends this when you see them."

Christiaan shook Sárá by the hair, and her head waved left and right. She gritted her teeth with pain but again made no sound.

"You are hurting Sárá, Christiaan," said Vulle. "This is not a good thing to do. I suggest that you release Sárá, and we can then let you be on your way. If you don't release Sárá, you will not be leaving this place. You cannot kill all of us. It doesn't matter how many friends you have in the cities. Here and now, you have too many enemies and too few friends."

Vulle's voice was calm, slow, and measured. There was a calm intensity and conviction behind what he said.

Christiaan paused. He was puzzled by the certainty in Vulle's voice.

The mist gathered thickly around the four people and the dogs. It was as if the world outside a ring ten paces wide did not exist. The only reality that existed was the tiny world in which these four people pitted their wits against one another.

"Enough. Idle chatting is over," said Christiaan. "Both of you move over there. I will take the sled and dogs. As long as I hear nothing from your military, I will leave Sárá in a safe place, and you will hear no more from me. I have more friends in Tromsø and Oslo than you think, Vulle. Even your precious police are not perfect saints." As he said this, he pointed the rifle to his right, to indicate that Vulle and Everton should move aside from their sled.

There was silence for a few moments. This was a stalemate. Vulle and Everton did not want to move too far from the dogs, but they could not risk rushing Christiaan and increasing the risk to Sárá.

Very slowly Vulle started to walk over the ice in the direction indicated by Christiaan. Everton started walking in the same direction, keeping a few paces away from Vulle as he did so.

Once both Everton and Vulle were ten paces from the dogs, Christiaan brought the rifle up to his right shoulder. In doing so, he released Sárá's hair and brought his left hand up to steady the stock of rifle. The rifle was aimed directly at Vulle's cape, but Sárá was now free.

Christiaan's movements were calm and unhurried. He clearly planned to shoot Vulle first.

The split second that Sárá's hair was released, she did not hesitate. It was as if she had been expecting this. She turned towards Christiaan, reached up, grabbed the barrel of the rifle with both of her hands, and lifted both feet off the ground. This happened very fast and caught Christiaan by surprise. The barrel lowered with Sárá's weight. As it lowered, the rifle barrel passed in front of her face.

This downwards movement of the rifle barrel took less than one second.

The wolf waiting just outside the ring of mist was ready too. He had hunted tens of thousands of times, over countless centuries. He was a skilled athlete. He had honed his hunting skills against creatures that were far more dangerous than humans. He had made mistakes in his very long life, but he had learned from these mistakes. As a result, he had become a very lethal hunter and killer. His timing and balance more than made up for any difference in size or strength of an opponent. He was fully aware of what was happening between the humans. He knew even before Vulle and Everton had arrived that there would come a moment of extreme danger for Sárá. A moment in which the difference between death and survival would be measured in milliseconds and in small forces applied at exactly the correct place and angle to unbalance his opponent. He had been through this sort of contest so many times that he was still very calm, and the pace of his heart was still even and slow when the moment for action arrived.

Although the humans could not see him, he knew exactly where they were. He detected the tensing of Christiaan's right arm before the rifle moved. He also detected the relaxation of Christiaan's left arm before Sárá's hair was released. The wolf knew Sárá well enough to know exactly what choice she would make. He was expecting her to pull the weapon to protect her father. Having travelled from a place outside human understanding, and having observed Sárá for many months, he considered Sárá to be a very competent and worthy warrior. He expected no less of her. Her small size and lack of physical strength meant nothing to him. He recognised and admired in her the rare qualities of a great hunter.

The wolf had started running before Christiaan was even aware that he was going to shoot Vulle. The wolf's paws were soundless on the soft layer of snow lying on the flat ice. It took only six of the wolf's long strides between his starting position and Christiaan. Christiaan was completely unaware of the wolf approaching until it was too late.

Everton and Vulle only became aware of the wolf as he emerged from the mist to the right of Christiaan. The rifle was swinging round towards Vulle as the wolf emerged, already running, silently but very fast. The wolf launched himself into a leap when he was ten feet from Christiaan.

Sárá was aware of the wolf. She had been aware that he was following her and Christiaan for some kilometres. Indeed, she was a little surprised that he had not followed them when they first left the cabins. She had also been aware that the wolf kept watching her when she was outside the cabins. She had seen his paw marks, as had her father, around the cabins. She knew that this wolf was not a normal wolf. He did not seem to bother the reindeer or the dogs, which was unusual. It was as if he could make himself invisible to them when he wished. His paw prints and the spacing of his paws was significantly larger than any wolf she had ever seen. She had caught sight of him once or twice. A movement in the forest, or the red reflection from his eyes, very briefly, while walking around the camp in the permanent arctic darkness, as had happened when she was with Jean. Each time she saw him, it was only for a fleeting second. She had the sense that he was allowing her to see him intermittently, that he was actually warning her or possibly reassuring her by his presence. In any case, she knew he was an ally and not a threat. This was partly why she knew she had to get the rifle away from her father. She was very confident that the wolf would help her to protect her father.

Vulle and Everton were powerless to influence events. The contest was between Christiaan with his rifle, Sárá, and a wolf.

Christiaan's trigger finger squeezed the rifle trigger as the barrel was level with Sárá's left eye. The wolf saw that this was about to happen. He knew enough about human weapons to know what resulted after the trigger was pulled. His vision detected even the most minute contraction of Christiaan's index finger. He knew that the barrel had to be moved away from Sárá's head. But he also knew that the barrel must not be moved so far that it returned to point at Vulle. He knew that bullets entering human flesh produced very serious results, which were irreversible, even for those with powers such as his people. The essence of the issue was the speed and force of his impact on Christiaan's left arm and the rifle barrel.

As the wolf flew through the air, his teeth closed on Christiaan's left wrist where it supported the rifle barrel and on the rifle barrel itself. At exactly the moment that the wolf's teeth closed on his arm, Christiaan's right index finger was pulling the trigger. At that moment precisely, as if she knew this was the right moment, Sárá released her hold on the rifle barrel and started to fall the few inches towards the ice. In the few milliseconds that it took for the primer in the rifle bullet to explode and the propellant to ignite, the wolf's jaws easily crushed both bones in Christiaan's forearm, near to the wrist. The force of the impact from the wolf started to push Christiaan's arm and the rifle barrel to Sárá's left. It took less than one thousandth of a second for the rifle barrel to move three inches to Sárá's left from its starting position. During that time, her head had fallen an inch. It took two thousandths of a second for the bullet to move from the chamber to the end of the rifle barrel.

As the bullet emerged from the rifle barrel, the power of the wolf's jaws continued to press on the barrel. The momentum of the wolf continued to push Christiaan's arm and rifle to Christiaan's right, and Sárá's head continued to fall.

From Vulle and Everton's perspective, things happened both very quickly but also in slow motion.

They were both suddenly aware that Sárá had grabbed the rifle barrel. Almost simultaneously they became aware that a large animal had emerged from the mist to the right of Christiaan, travelling very fast. Indeed, the animal seemed to be flying through the air at the point when he emerged from the mist. There was a collision between the animal and Christiaan, and almost simultaneously a detonation and flash from the rifle. Sárá's fur hat flew off, and Sárá fell onto the ice. Christiaan also fell to the ice, with the wolf still clamped to his left forearm. As Christiaan hit the ice, the wolf released his grip. The rifle clattered onto the ice and spun away from Christiaan. The force of the impact sent Christiaan sliding backwards. The wolf landed on its feet expertly and turned through 180 degrees despite the slippery ice. He came to a halt facing towards Christiaan, ready to pounce again if necessary.

As Christiaan slid on the ice, there was an ominous cracking sound from the ice beneath him. He had been pushed towards the dark, thin area of ice. The ice where he lay was only millimetres thick and could not support his body. Freezing water started to bubble up around him.

The collision of forces lasted less than half a second.

Vulle and Everton were frozen in shock for a further second.

By the end of the encounter, the rifle was disabled, with the barrel crushed, and separated from Christiaan; Sárá lay still on the ice, without her hat; Christiaan was separated from both his rifle and Sárá; and the wolf stood calmly, staring at Christiaan.

Vulle launched himself towards the limp figure of Sárá lying on the ice.

A small pool of blood was spreading from her head, staining the white ice and the powdery layer of snow a shocking red. Vulle knelt next to Sárá and lifted her head and shoulders into his lap. She did not respond as he spoke her name.

The wolf remained still, staring at the hapless form of Christiaan. Christiaan whimpered and tried to move both of his arms to stay afloat. His left hand and wrist were extended at an unnatural angle. Blood was gushing from his left sleeve and spurting into the freezing water that now surrounded him.

Everton moved towards the rifle. The barrel was deformed and crushed beyond repair. That particular rifle would not threaten Sárá again.

The ice around Christiaan was fragmenting with each of his movements. Christiaan kicked his feet and thrashed his right arm in an attempt to move to thicker ice. His attempts were fruitless, as more ice broke and more water appeared around him. Within seconds, a large hole in the ice surrounded Christiaan. He was sinking into the frigid water. He shouted something unintelligible and reached for the edge of solid ice with his one good hand. He was just able to reach the solid ice. His right hand slid over the ice each time he tried to gain purchase. As he struggled, he slid slowly deeper into the water. His clothes were becoming waterlogged and were pulling him down faster.

The wolf watched Christiaan sink slowly into the lake. Everton became aware of the danger for Christiaan and looked around for something to use to pull him out of the water. The only available tool was the broken rifle. Everton grabbed the rifle by the stock and swung it round to offer the barrel for Christiaan to cling to. The wolf watched Everton and stepped back, away from Christiaan. It was as if the wolf did not want to play any part in a rescue of Christiaan but he was not willing to prevent it.

Christiaan was now submerged up to his neck in freezing water. He was also bleeding from a shattered left arm. The combination of low temperatures and loss of blood was impairing the blood supply to his upper body. His vision had become white, and he was no longer aware of his surroundings. Everton thrust the rifle towards Christiaan. The ice around Everton's feet moved slightly, and he heard some cracking as pieces came loose.

"Take hold of the rifle," shouted Everton.

Christiaan did not seem to hear. Everton watched as Christiaan's head slowly sank into the arctic water. Bubbles emerged from his open mouth, and his head disappeared quickly from view into the black depths of the lake.

Everton carefully moved back from the area where Christiaan had fallen through the ice.

As soon as Christiaan disappeared, the wolf walked towards Vulle, who was cradling Sárá in his lap. Blood was running from her head onto his thick fur trousers. The wolf paused, looked into Vulle's eyes, and lowered its head, as if asking for his consent to approach closer.

Vulle did not move. He looked at the wolf, and tears ran down his cheeks.

The wolf stepped slowly forwards. Its nose approached Sárá's face. It seemed to be sniffing or possibly looking very closely at Sárá.

Sárá's eyes opened. She looked at the wolf and smiled. She lifted her right hand and touched the side of the wolf's head. The wolf seemed to press its head into her hand.

Vulle and Everton remained silent and still during this exchange between Sárá and the wolf.

Very slowly, the wolf walked backwards several steps. He raised his head, looked at Vulle for a brief moment, then turned calmly and walked away into the mist, back in the direction from which he had arrived.

Sárá sat up and put her hand to her left temple. Blood was still leaking from the skin above her left ear.

Vulle was speechless.

"I am OK, Daddy," said Sárá. "You don't need to squeeze me so tight. You will stop me breathing. But I can't hear in my left ear. It is ringing."

Sárá rubbed her left ear, and her hand came away covered in blood.

Vulle pulled out a small cloth from one of his many pockets and dabbed at Sárá's temple. Her white-blond hair was matted with blood. There was a shallow, two-inch graze above her left ear. The judgment of the wolf had not been perfect, just nearly perfect. The bullet had removed a thin line of Sárá's skin on her left temple but otherwise had caused no permanent harm. Sárá carried a small scar over her left ear for the rest of her long and successful life.

Vulle pressed the cloth to Sárá's temple and pulled her in to hug her tightly again, kissing the top of her head. Sárá hugged Vulle back, and the two sat on the ice and snow in a puddle of red blood for several minutes.

Vulle fashioned a bandage for Sárá's head with some cloth torn from spare clothing in their pack. By the time her bandage was tied, she was standing and chatting to the two older men as if nothing exceptional had happened.

"Daddy, look at your cape," said Sárá.

Vulle looked down at his woollen cape. It was stained with blood.

"Look, Daddy. There is a hole there," said Sárá.

She approached Vulle and pushed her finger through a hole half an inch in diameter in the front of his cape. She then pushed her finger through a matching hole in the back of it. He spread out his arms. The two holes were in the right side of his cape.

"The bullet passed through your cape, between your arm and your side," said Sárá. "You were very lucky. That man could have killed you."

"I don't think it was luck," said Vulle. "You saved me. With some help from your special friend."

"What sort of wolf was that?" said Everton, looking to where the wolf tracks disappeared into the mist. "It was the size of a small cow."

"It was a very special wolf," said Sárá. "It was following us for quite some time."

"You knew that it was following us?" said Everton.

"I told you it was leading us, or protecting us, since we left Camp Arktis," said Sárá. "You should believe me when I tell you these things, Mr. Everton. This is our world now. We are not in London, like Mr. Sherlock Holmes, with everything logical and rational. There are different rules in the world of the Sami."

Sárá smiled at Everton. Vulle smiled at Sárá. Everton smiled back at Sárá. They all laughed.

The dogs had been standing and sitting silently by the sled since they had arrived, no more than ten minutes previously. They knew from the voices and smells that their humans had been on serious business until now. With the laughter and the change of odour, they detected the change in mood and started yelping and barking, hoping that another run might be possible.

Vulle stood and looked at the hole in the ice where Christiaan had disappeared.

"This is quite rare," said Vulle. "Lake ice at this time of year is very thick. Ten inches or more. Christiaan was unlucky that he ran out of fuel so close to a patch of such thin ice. We are lucky that he didn't drive the snowmobile over the thin ice and into the lake. That would have been the end of him and Sárá."

Sárá also looked at the hole in the ice. "This is not a natural hole in the ice, Daddy. Something unnatural has caused this hole. I think this was planned long before we arrived here."

"I think I remember you saying there could be a small geo-thermal vent at the bottom of the lake," said Everton. "Or even a new volcano forming. I think that is a more plausible natural theory for the thin ice. As you told us, geothermal activity is known all over Scandinavia."

Sárá shook her head.

"I don't think we will ever know for sure how all this happened," said Vulle.

CHAPTER 15

Huginn

NOW THAT THE DANGER had passed, Vulle, Sárá, and Everton all felt the cold that surrounded them. They stashed the broken rifle on the sled. Sárá placed her fur hat over her red-and-white bandage. Everton sat on the sled, and Sárá sat in front of him with the bearskin rug over her legs.

Vulle stood on the footboard and released the claw brake.

Čammo, the lead dog, instinctively knew that they were returning to camp. He yelped at the other dogs and jumped into action almost before Vulle gave the command. Čammo had watched the wolf in combat and knew that he was in the presence of a truly fearsome predator. Čammo respected the wolf but was relieved when it chose to depart.

The dogs took the sled in a wide circle, well clear of the hole in the ice, and they retraced their tracks east towards the forest, the mountain pass, and Camp Trollfjell. They had been without food for half a day. The dogs and the men had been running almost continuously for many hours. It was almost midnight. Yet the dogs were full of energy and delighted to pull their humans as fast as their legs could travel.

The freezing mist thinned as they rose towards the mountain pass and eventually cleared completely. The velvety black sky yawned above them. A path of stars sprinkled across the sky from horizon to horizon. As they crested the rise of the pass, as if by magic, the ribbons of glorious green, blue, yellow, and pink lights lit up above them and danced backwards and forwards. Despite the deadly events of the past hours, all three of them gazed at the lights in awe. This time even Everton thought he could hear a slight whispering from the lights. Perhaps he imagined it.

The wolf who had saved Sárá was long gone. He had travelled a great distance by the time they reached the mountain pass and looked down on the plain leading to Camp Trollfjell. His job was done, and he was confident that the charge of keeping Sárá safe was assured. He returned to his people, using paths that are unknown to most men.

But eyes were still on Sárá and her companions. A large raven flew lazily on a parallel path to the sled. It was at least a kilometre away most of the time, but it could see every hair of the fur on Sárá's reindeer-skin hat. Through its eyes, its master was assured that Sárá remained safe, to return to her family and resume her quest for knowledge. The cold and dark were as nothing to this unusual creature.

As the sled passed down the valley and entered the forested plains, several arctic predators were aware of the passing group. Without knowing it, the humans passed a couple of foxes, a pack of wolves resting after a successful kill, and several wolverines sniffing for food. The dogs and the wild animals were all aware of the powerful flying creature that looked like a raven and was travelling with them. But they all knew that it had powers beyond those of the natural world. The wild predators knew to stay clear of this flying creature and the dangerous human travellers.

By the time the dogs pulled them into Camp Trollfjell, it was three o'clock in the morning. Edo, Oskár, and Ánne heard the dogs approach. They were hardly sleeping, or sleeping very lightly, while Sárá was in danger. All three of them quickly threw on their warm fur coats and hats and ran out to greet the returning group.

Oskár and Ánne ran to Sárá and smothered her in hugs. Ánne asked Sárá about her head, looking with concern at the bloodstained bandage. Sárá stood like a tiny furry Buddha and explained what had happened in a rapid and high-pitched Sami story, acting out the most exciting parts in front of them. They both stood with open mouths in astonishment, in the snow, as the story unfolded.

Vulle and Edo unharnessed the dogs and gave them a feed before they curled up in their boxes for a well-earned rest.

Edo was very interested in the crushed and mangled rifle barrel. Vulle showed Edo the bullet holes that had penetrated his cape without even scratching him. Edo shook his head in astonishment at Vulle's narrow escape.

Before they separated to sleep, Vulle walked up and threw his hands around Everton. This was quite difficult because Everton was almost a foot taller than Vulle. But Vulle had wide shoulders and managed quite a good bear hug.

Vulle stepped back, placed his hands on Everton's shoulders, and looked directly into his eyes. "I thank you for your help this night. You are a good friend to my family. I owe you a great deal, and if I can ever repay the debt, I will," said Vulle.

Sárá also walked to Everton through the thick snow and threw her arms around one of his legs. "Thank you for helping to save me and my daddy, Mr. Everton," she said in a small voice.

"You are all very welcome," said Everton, "but I think that wolf had the entire situation under control all the time somehow. I don't think I played much of a part. I felt like a spectator most of the time."

"We all had a part to play. There was risk for us all," said Vulle, patting Everton on the shoulder. "Sleep well."

They separated, and Everton walked to his cabin. As he was stamping the snow off his boots, Jean woke and came to greet him. She insisted on hearing the entire story, from beginning to end, and then wanted him to repeat several parts of it, just to make sure that she fully grasped the sequence of events.

"So, a mysterious wolf saved Sárá and magically protected Vulle from harm as well. And some unknown force took Christiaan into the frozen lake by melting and cracking ice that should have been ten inches thick," said Jean. "For now, I will just about accept our interpretation of all this at face value, without trying to explain too much. However, there is another thing that is puzzling me. You and Vulle visiting this cabin in the wilds, and the Dutch group disappearing. Are these things linked? Where are the two other Dutch tourists? What exactly is going on between you and Vulle?"

Everton yawned. "Jean, I am exhausted. I need a decent sleep. It is nearly four o'clock in the morning. Let's sleep. In the morning when we wake, I am sure that everything will become clear. I am expecting to hear from Vulle's cousin, Sofe. She should have some useful information for us about the blood tests."

Everton was pulling his boots off as he said this. As soon as his parka and overtrousers were off, he fell back on the bed and closed his eyes.

Jean shook her head and watched him lying pretending to sleep. She knew better than to insist. There would be time for explanations later.

As Sárá and her family walked to their cabin, the raven that had followed them watched unseen from the top of the tallest pine tree in the surrounding forest. He bowed his head and wiped his beak on the pine branch. His bright eyes twinkled as he looked at the humans.

CHAPTER 16

Sofe

EVEN THOUGH THE TRAVELLERS did not get to bed until after four o'clock, they were all awake by seven o'clock.

Before they went for breakfast, Jean insisted on an explanation from Everton. "Tell me what has been going on. From the beginning," she said.

"OK. What do you want to know?" said Everton.

"What is the link between you and Vulle?"

"Well, firstly, I have to admit now that this trip was always a mixture of business and pleasure."

"You mean you have been working with Vulle while we have been on this arctic safari?"

"Partly. Yes. Partly yes."

"Go on," said Jean.

"Back in England, I have been working for several years with the English drug trafficking people and the Norwegian police to tackle a ring of drug smugglers. We knew for some time that drugs were leaving England in ferries from Newcastle Upon Tyne, via Bergen, arriving in Tromsø. We wanted to find out how they distributed their drugs from Tromsø. Christiaan and his friends were working for these drug smugglers. We knew they were booked on a trip to Camp Trollfjell. It was convenient for us to enjoy a similar trip to Camp Trollfjell as well. That way Vulle and I could keep an eye on what they were doing."

"Vulle too. Vulle and you have been working with the Norwegian police?"

"Ah, yes. Vulle was my contact in the Sami community. He has been in on this thing since the beginning. Vulle has a role in the Norwegian police force. This is not widely known. You might say he has an undercover role. I actually met Vulle when we visited the Tromsø police station when we first arrived here. You might recall that visit to the police station."

"So, you and Vulle have actually been working all this time, while you pretended to be on holiday with me."

"Yes, that's one way of describing it. But we were genuinely having a holiday too, weren't we? I wasn't pretending about that."

"And who else knew about all of this?" said Jean. "Did Vulle's family know? Am I the last one to know?"

"Edo is also on the payroll of the Norwegian police."

"And?"

"I think that Vulle's family are aware of his police duties."

"What? All of them? Sárá and Oskár included?"

"I believe so."

"So that's why they appeared unconcerned when you and Vulle were away overnight visiting the military base and the cabin in the woods," said Jean. "And what about Beth, Henry, Rolf and his wife? Were they all in on this escapade of yours?"

"No. The rest of our fellow travellers are just tourists. Henry's illness was an unexpected complication. And Rolf's attempts to have Henry sent into the wilderness were just a bit of a crazy diversion."

"What exactly did you find in the cabin in the woods?" said Jean.

"Ah, right. Yes. Well, we knew where Christiaan and his friends were going on their snowmobiles, which were all tracked. They were visiting the same cabin repeatedly. Edo and Vulle just allowed them freedom to roam, which would not be normal with tourists, obviously. It would be far too dangerous to let tourists get lost in temperatures so far below zero. When Vulle and I got to the cabin, we found a stash of what is almost certainly cocaine there. Many hundreds of kilograms of a class-A drug at least. It seems that Christiaan and the others were using the stories about the cabin being haunted to ensure that nobody visited their stash. Once the cocaine landed in Tromsø, it appears it was being taken cross country to the cabin and hidden. From there, it could be distributed around northern Scandinavia when authorities were not looking. The porous, or nonexistent, borders up here helped this flow of drugs, of course. Christiaan and his friends were couriers moving shipments of drugs from what is called 'the inhospitable cabin' to various secluded sites in Russia, Finland, and Sweden, as dead drops for local distributors. The concealed tracking devices on their snowmobiles gave us precise locations for their drops. Their role was to distribute the drugs from the Halti Mountain area into the other countries. This explains their repeated trips for many hours each day. We let Vulle's relative, Sofe, know about this. She is in contact with the authorities in other countries. Somehow, Christiaan must have evaded capture and managed to get back to Camp Trollfjell. You know the rest."

"And what happened to the two other Dutch 'tourists' with Christiaan?" said Jean.

"I am still not sure. Vulle was working with both the Norwegian police and the Norwegian army on this project," said Everton. "Vulle was regularly in contact with his cousin, Sofe. As soon as we found the cocaine, we informed Sofe. She arranged for appropriate surveillance and forensic testing at the scene. For this, her access to military transport helicopters was important, especially with the roads being closed during the heavy snowfall. We might find out more from Sofe later about the other two Dutch couriers. After eluding capture, Christiaan just needed to get far enough away to evade the police and the military. If he had managed to take our dogs and our sled, he would have been free because there was no tracker on the dogsled Vulle and I were using. It was a close shave on the frozen lake. We were lucky in many ways."

"Will they recover Christiaan's body from the lake?"

"Probably. But they will need to wait until the spring thaw. Once the ice melts, they can dive in the lake. Hopefully they will find his body."

"OK. Let's get our breakfast," said Jean, standing and pulling on her coat and gloves.

Everton knew he wasn't out of the woods with Jean yet. There would be a reckoning for running a covert work project during their northern lights holiday. But for now, Jean was taking all this very calmly. Perhaps too calmly.

Jean and Everton sat with Sárá and Oskár at the breakfast table. Sárá had a neat and clean bandage wrapped around her head. She appeared to have forgotten about it entirely and chatted merrily to Jean about the role of Severus Snape in Harry Potter's life.

As they ate breakfast, the throb of helicopter blades could be heard outside. A military helicopter flew over their camp, with lights illuminating the dark forest clearing. It landed in their clearing in a cloud of snow a couple hundred metres from the cabins. Reindeer grazing on the edge of the forest looked up at the noisy machine landing and disgorging its humans, then lowered their heads and continued the important task of eating.

Vulle went out to greet their military visitors. A few minutes later he popped his head back through the door of the dining cabin and beckoned to Everton. Vulle and Everton walked to Vulle's family lavvu, which he also used as his office in the camp.

In the lavvu, Major Sofe sat on the reindeer hides. Everton knew that the news she was bringing was good because there was no attempt to keep her distance. She wore no masks or gloves. She rose and shook his hand, then hugged him closely and introduced herself more informally than at their last meeting in the blizzard.

"We have achieved a good result all round," said Sofe. "We alerted the Russians to the fact that Willem was carrying drugs into their territory. Shortly afterwards, the tracking device on his snowmobile went silent. The Russians now deny any knowledge of his whereabouts. Either they have picked him up and he will vanish forever as punishment for his illegal smuggling activities, or they have picked him up to protect him and prevent him from revealing anything about Russian organised crime gangs. Yvette was tracked into Finland, and the Finnish authorities arrested her with her load of drugs on the snowmobile. The Finnish and Swedes have also picked up several additional contacts when they attempted to collect some of the illegal drugs that the three Dutch couriers dropped in each country. In Norway, we have also rounded up several Norwegians who delivered the drugs from the ship to the inhospitable cabin in the first place from Tromsø. Altogether we have disrupted their supply chain through this route from England into at least four arctic countries. A very good result.

"The trafficking route to and from England will be closed for the foreseeable future. We have also removed at least one distribution method in our country, and also in Finland, Sweden, and Russia. Several of the traffickers are behind bars, and one is dead, of course. So I want to thank you, Detective Everton, for your help with this operation. And also you, Vulle, and our family, for your service in this matter. I was very sorry to hear about little Sárá's injury. However, I understand that the injury was not serious and that she is expected to recover fully."

"Ja. Sárá will be fine, Sofe," said Vulle. "I think that the drug smugglers were in more danger from Sárá than the other way round."

"What do you make of the wolf that attacked Christiaan?" said Everton.

Sofe and Vulle looked at each other and paused before Sofe replied.

"Officially, of course, this was a lone wolf that attacked a man in the wilderness. This happens sometimes. We live with large predators. We must accept that people will occasionally be predated. We were lucky that the wolf attacked the 'right' person and saved the defenceless little girl from serious harm. The brave detective from England gets great credit for distracting the evil drug smuggler, which allowed the wolf to pounce. I will ensure that your superiors are notified of your valour in this matter," said Sofe with a wide smile.

"Mmm. I'm not sure I played any part in the solution," said Everton. "And the wolf was gigantic. As large as a small reindeer. You should have seen the speed with which it moved. And it only attacked Christiaan. It actually prevented Sárá being seriously injured. It also prevented Vulle from being shot. It was then very gentle with Sárá and appeared to be concerned about her. It was also perfectly calm with Vulle and me, in a manner that I would not expect of a wild animal. It almost seemed to understand what we were feeling and thinking," said Everton.

"Yes, all this may be true, Mr. Everton," said Sofe. "But we cannot ascribe supernatural forces to the animals in our country. That would be ridiculous, would it not? You are a rational man. A man of reason. You pursue your business in England based on evidence, logic, and reasoning. We, too, are rational people in Norway. So, what am I to say in my report? What is Vulle to write to his senior police officers in his report? It was not a wolf? It was some form of supernatural spirit that had supernatural powers? Of course it was a wolf. You saw it yourself. So did Sofe and Vulle. Some wolves are big, and some are smaller. These are not amazing things. Sárá was clearly very fortunate not to be seriously injured or even killed. But the wolf cannot have known what it was doing in terms of protecting Sárá. Or could it? What will you write in your report in England, Mr. Everton? That a wolf spirit being flew out of the mist and saved your lives while killing a drug trafficker? How would you explain that to your senior officers in England? I don't think they are very familiar with the Norse legends of Freki the wolf, who acts as Odin's agent, or the Sami wolf-man Stuorra-Jovna, who can turn into a wolf at will, or Suologievra the wolf spirit who can travel between the lower, middle, and upper worlds. What will your prime minister think if he reads about supernatural spirits helping the English police in Sami country? He will think that we have been feeding you too much Akavit and your brain has turned to mush."

Vulle smiled as he listened to Sofe, then laughed softly and patted Everton on the shoulder.

"Right. Yes. Of course. In terms of the official reports, it must have been a random wolf attack, combined with a great deal of good luck. I think we are all agreed on that," said Everton.

Vulle smiled again and clapped Everton on the back. "We must tell our seniors what they want to hear. We are used to that, Everton, aren't we?"

"Now, I have some news about the tests on Mr. Henry Gibson and about the infectious disease outbreaks in London and New York," said Sofe. "I would like to tell Henry Gibson first and then give this news to all your guests together, Vulle. Could you get Mr. Gibson first, and then we can clear all this up."

Vulle went out and soon returned with Henry Gibson. After a brief conversation with Henry, Sofe stood in her white winter coat, and all four of them walked across the snow to the dining cabin.

As they entered the cabin, the conversation among the breakfasters fizzled out. All faces turned to face them expectantly. Henry sat next to his wife, smiling broadly.

"Good morning, everyone," said Sofe. "I have some news I wanted to give to you all together. I am Major Sofe Issaksdatter. I work at the local military base at Helligskogen, as the camp medical officer. Firstly, some very good news. I have received confirmation from the Norwegian government that the travel restrictions have all been lifted. Everyone is free to travel again without any restraint. It turns out that the two outbreaks of infection in New York and London were completely unrelated.

One was caused by a mistake at a research laboratory in England. The New York cluster was in a group of travellers from South America. The infectious agents were different strains of a similar virus. There is no evidence that anyone else has been affected or that there has been any further spread of infection. The World Health Organization and the authorities in England and America have lifted their recommendations about travel bans. Our snow ploughs are clearing our roads in Norway. Once you all get back to Camp Arktis, you will find that your road transport is available to take you all back to Tromsø. I am so pleased to bring you this news."

There was a muted cheer from all the tourists. The Italian children clapped enthusiastically. Rolf and his wife, Ulva, hugged each other. Rolf's nose was bandaged, and bruises encircled both of his eyes. Henry put his arm around Beth's shoulder and kissed her head.

"I also have some tests back on Mr. Henry Gibson, which confirm that he did not have any form of infection. I have Mr. Gibson's permission to tell this to you. Mr. Gibson has a rare blood disorder that produces a special type of antibodies in very cold weather. These antibodies are called cold agglutinins. They can cause very severe illness, and even death, in very cold weather. Henry was completely unaware of this condition until he visited our chilly Norwegian region. This is not an infectious disease. You cannot catch it from someone else. It is inherited. Many people never know they have this condition if they live in a warmer climate. Mr. Gibson has now fully recovered. Indeed, he has made a much more rapid recovery than I would have expected. For this, I am sure he has to thank the care of Vulle's family. As long as he is careful to prevent his extremities from getting cold, he should not suffer any more illness. I am sure he is very grateful to everyone in this camp for their concern and support when he was ill."

Sofe paused and stared directly at Rolf. There was silence from all the tourists. Henry beamed. Beth smiled almost as widely.

"Anyway, I hope this reassures those among you who might have thought that Henry's illness was linked in any way to the events in London and New York," said Sofe. "I hope you all enjoy the rest of your stay in Camp Trollfjell."

Vulle escorted Sofe out of the cabin and across the snow to her waiting helicopter.

Back in the dining cabin, the tourists started to disperse. It was their last day at Camp Trollfjell.

Henry and Beth approached Everton and Jean as they sat at their table.

"We are hitching a ride back to Camp Arktis on a spare snowmobile. It will be quicker and safer for me," said Henry. "With the Dutch youngsters out of the frame, Edo can cope with a couple of ancient Americans. Thanks to both of you for your help on the way out here and while I was ill."

"No problem, Henry," said Jean. "We are only too happy to have been able to help. It sounds like Florida is the right place for you to live. People with cold agglutinin haemolytic anaemia should probably avoid the Arctic as much as possible."

Henry scratched his head and nodded. "You are one hundred percent right there, Jean. I know it now. We won't be visiting northern latitudes again in a hurry."

Sárá was sitting at the table with Jean and Everton. Henry turned to Sárá, lifted her off the seat, and smothered her in a huge bear hug.

"I need to thank you especially, young lady. Without your help, I don't think I would have found my way back here from… from wherever I had gone. I will never forget my dream. I will never forget meeting you when you were older too. You are going to go far," said Henry.

"You are most welcome, Mr. Gibson," said Sárá. "It was you who made the necessary choices. I think my role was just to make sure you knew what choices were available, psychologically speaking."

"If you or your family are ever down our way in Florida, you should look us up. We will be able to show you the delights of a very different climate and culture, fifty degrees warmer and fifty degrees closer to the equator," said Beth.

The trip back to Camp Arktis for Jean and Everton was less eventful than the trip out. The dogs were just as keen to run. The snow was just as deep. Vulle and Sárá shared their sleds. Ánne and Oskár stayed with the reindeer at Camp Trollfjell. They did hear some wolves calling, but they were far off in the mountains. Sárá was also aware of a large raven that seemed to be ahead of them the entire journey. Everywhere they stopped for a rest, the same raven seemed to be perched on the highest pine tree, waiting for them and watching them with shiny eyes.

They made good time and arrived at Camp Arktis by late afternoon. It was December 28.

CHAPTER 17

Oslo

JEAN AND EVERTON TRAVELLED back to Tromsø on December 29, sharing the minibus with the other tourists.

Edo drove the minibus. Sárá and Vulle travelled with them. Sárá sat with Jean, and Vulle sat next to Everton. As they sped through the dark arctic morning, above them the aurora crackled into life. Multicoloured ribbons of light rippled and combined in the sky.

"Look at that display," said Jean. "We have seen the northern lights almost every day since we arrived in Norway. It's fantastic every time I see it."

"Yes, for me too," said Sárá. "I don't get used to it. It is always amazing."

"You can see how people thought it was something super-natural. It looks like nothing else we encounter," said Jean. "The story about Bivrost being the magical road to the home of the gods would have seemed a plausible theory before we knew about astrophysics."

Sárá and Jean stared out of the minibus window at the snow fields, the dark winter sky, and the spectacular light display.

"OK," said Sárá. "But this is not a story, actually. I mean, it is a story, but it is a true story. Bivrost is another name for the northern lights, which is really a bridge that connects the land of men with the land of the gods. This is true. It is not a Norse myth. Other bridges and paths also connect the other lands of the Viking world.

"There is a Norse poem, 'Grímnismál,' in which the universe is centred on the trunk of a magical tree named Yggdrasil. This magical tree will be the meeting place of the gods when the world ends and Ragnarok engulfs the world with flames. This is a Norse reference to climate-change activists, of course. Our ancestors knew that climate was always changing and would always be changing and that climate activists would be coming once we stopped having to worry about feeding ourselves so much. The tree has three main roots that connect parts of the universe. One root connects the human world to the tree, another one goes to the giant-lands, and a third one descends towards the kingdom Hel, the goddess of death. Did you know, Jean, that the English word *hell* is derived from the Norse word *hel*, meaning a hidden place? These magical tree roots are a bit like the Bivrost too, you see. Two versions of the same story. Magical roads to heaven. Humans like stories about getting to heaven, don't they? Now, I wonder why that is.

"Anyway, Yggdrasil's three roots, despite being quite logically gigantic, are under the constant attack of an evil snake, Nidhöggr, who constantly chews on them. This is possibly another metaphor for climate change destroying our ecosystems. These greenies get everywhere. At the other end of the magic tree, high up in the clouds where the highest branches of the tree reach, lives a fabulous eagle. The eagle really hates the snake who is threatening his wooden perch, and he spends most of his time shouting insults at it. To take these inventive insults to Niddöggr below, the eagle uses Ratatoskr, a magical squirrel, as a messenger. This squirrel constantly runs up and down the world tree to take insults to Nidhöggr and to take insulting answers back up the tree. This is a metaphor for most human interactions. Your poet Shakespeare described this in his Scottish play. He said that life is a tale, told by a fool, full of sound and fury, signifying nothing. This is another way for describing that most of our lives are wasted fighting one another in pointless battles. In Scotland, this was true back then. Did you know that some people believe there are some Sami people in Scotland too? That is close to your home in England, isn't it, Jean?" Sárá stopped to catch her breath.

"Yes, Sárá, Scotland is just north of England," said Jean. "We live a hundred miles south of the border with Scotland. You might have some relatives there, I suppose."

Sárá nodded in agreement, then resumed her tale. "Now, in the kingdom of Hel, dead people who did not die in battle stay after death. According to the medieval Icelandic poet with the wonderful name of Snorri Sturluson, when the god Baldur was killed, his brother Hermóðr rode for nine nights and nine days to the dreary land of Hel. When he arrived there, he was met with a massive river that could only be crossed by walking over a magical bridge. The bridge, called the Gjállabrú, is like the Bivrost in reverse. It is guarded by a female giant named Móðgugr and is covered and thatched with shimmering gold.

"There is also an ancient Sami tale of a counsellor who waits for all the lost souls at the gates of Hel. She talks to the people before they enter Hel. If she can change the way they think enough, so that they think only good thoughts and have only positive feelings, then they can go to heaven instead of Hel. The counsellor's name in the story is…Jean Sárásvenn. This means

'Jean, friend of Sárá' in English. What a remarkable coincidence, don't you think, Jean?"

Sárá halted her tale and looked at Jean's face for a reaction. Jean smiled and nodded in agreement.

"I'm going to miss you, Jean," said Sárá. "You have taught me a lot about psychology."

"Really?" said Jean. "I wasn't aware that I was teaching you at all. If anything, I think you taught me a great deal on this trip. You have been a revelation to us. You have a brilliant mind. You must use it well."

"Did you enjoy your arctic safari with us?" said Sárá.

"I enjoyed most of it. I was very worried that you might be hurt when Christiaan took you with him. I should have known that he was really the one who was in danger. He should have known better than to mess with the mighty Sárá and her spirit wolf companion."

"You are so nice to me, Jean. I wish I could take you home with me forever," said Sárá, hugging Jean's arm tightly and leaning her head on Jean.

"That's nice," said Jean. "You should come and see us in England. You can visit us anytime. But you have a wonderful family. You should enjoy them and the wonderful country you live in. You are very lucky to have all this."

The two girlfriends talked on for several hours. Sometime later the minibus pulled into their destination outside the tour operator's office in Tromsø.

The tourists all alighted from the bus. As Sárá stepped off the bus, she spotted a small elderly lady standing a few paces away.

"*Bestemor,*" shouted Sárá. She ran towards the old lady and wrapped her in a hug. The old lady returned the hug and kissed

Sárá on the top of her head. The old lady and Sárá talked for a few seconds in Sami. Sárá turned and pointed towards Jean and Everton as they spoke. Then Sárá took the old lady's hand and pulled her towards Jean.

"This is my granny, Jean," said Sárá. "I want you to meet her. She is a great Sami healer and hunter. She hunts criminals, not animals."

The old lady beamed a smile at Jean and Everton and extended her hand. "Good afternoon, Detective and Mrs. Everton," said the old lady. "I am Kristin Olsen, Tromsø chief of police—and Sárá's granny too, of course."

She shook both of their hands formally. She was hardly more than five feet tall, with very short grey hair and light blue eyes. She was wearing a full police uniform.

"I want to thank you in person for the help you have given us in Tromsø to combat the drug traffickers. Without your help, we would not have been nearly as successful. And I want to thank you for helping to keep my little Sárá safe."

"Thank you, Ms. Olsen," said Everton. "I am happy that the operation went so well. And I was very happy to do the very little that I was able to help Sárá. It was really Sárá keeping us all safe, you know."

Jean smiled and nodded. "I think we met when we first arrived at the airport and then again possibly when we bought my husband's hat," she said.

"Ja, I wanted to meet the people who were travelling with my son and my precious granddaughter. I was very happy with what I saw. I knew then that Sárá was safe with you. Have a safe journey, and thank you again for your help," said Ms. Olsen.

Sárá looked slightly puzzled by the fact that her granny and the Evertons had already met, but she shrugged and accepted it.

"Sárá's granny was the lady who helped you with your luggage at the airport," said Jean as she and Everton walked through the hotel lobby on the way to their room. "And she was also in the hat shop in Tromsø on our first day here."

"Yep. She was checking us out," said Everton.

"Well, that is interesting," said Jean.

"I think Sárá and her granny are two peas in a pod," said Everton. "And granny is also the Tromsø police chief. That is something I didn't know until now."

The next day Jean and Everton flew south to Oslo. They stayed one night. While they were there, they visited the Norwegian National Museum of Art. Everton had a habit of visiting galleries on their travels, usually with Jean.

"We always seem to end up at the gallery, wherever we travel," said Jean as they walked along the cobbled street approaching the gallery.

The streetlights cast a warm glow on the cobbles. Snow was heaped up, clearing a path for the commuters and visitor. The cobbles were outlined in white and pale grey. It was well below zero, and they both still needed multiple layers of warm clothing in the capital.

"Yes. Strange, isn't it?" said Everton. "Nothing to do with me. It just seems to happen without either of us making a decision. Perhaps it is the Sami spirit of art in Oslo pushing us along the streets without our knowledge."

"You might just be right about that," said Jean.

Everton's habit whenever he visited a gallery was to walk through all the rooms at a steady pace, without stopping at any particular painting, just trying to identify which paintings caught his eye naturally. After visiting all the rooms, he would then retrace his steps and spend much longer studying one or two paintings that had caught his attention that day. He found that the paintings that most interested him varied from day to day, and from visit to visit, in any particular gallery.

It was New Year's Eve, and they had just completed an arctic safari in the wilderness and mountains of Norway. They were attuned to the permanent darkness and the ubiquitous covering of snow, which coloured everything with a palette of grey, purple, and blue in the arctic winter.

Jean was used to Everton's routine and went along with him during their gallery trips.

After his first circuit in the gallery, Everton made straight for a picture of a winter landscape.[1] The gallery was not very busy, and he and Jean had an unobstructed view from a vacant wooden seat in the centre of the room.

"This is a woodcut on paper," said Everton. "The whole scene is in two colours, black and white. The woodcut technique, with black ink on white paper, lends itself to the starkness of the landscape in the winter in the permanent arctic darkness. How does it make you feel?"

Jean studied the small picture for a couple of minutes. "On the one hand, it gives me a feeling of deep cold," she said. "It is a very cold scene. A hostile landscape that will freeze you to death if you don't have the right skills. On the other hand, I see the lights in the windows of the cabin, and it gives me a feeling of impending warmth and hospitality. It reminds me of the Sami people who looked after us so well. Their skills and knowledge were the difference between life and death out there, quite literally."

"Yes, I agree with all that," said Everton. "It is amazing how Munch manages to evoke all these feelings with just a few simple black lines on a piece of white paper. It shows that there must be a link between the artist's brain in 1898 and our brains nearly a hundred years later. We must be seeing beyond the white paper and black ink to a world that existed in Edvard Munch's head."

"Perhaps that was what we witnessed with Henry Gibson. Somehow Sárá was able to make a link between her thoughts and Henry's thoughts that none of the rest of us managed. She was able to see beyond simple external signs of illness and reach a deeper understanding of Henry's inner state. This might have allowed her to help change that state and therefore start the healing process."

"Mmm," said Everton, shaking his head. "Or perhaps Henry just got better once he warmed up."

They stood and walked to an adjacent room. They sat opposite another winter scene.

"This one is simply entitled 'Winter,'" said Jean, reading from a museum guide. "It's the same artist, Edvard Munch."[2]

"What do you feel with this one?" said Everton after they had both contemplated it for a couple of minutes.

"This has a softer feel," said Jean. "The snow still looks blue white and cold, but it has a gentle feel, as if it could envelop you and keep you insulated. The dark gaps between the tree trunks gives a slightly ominous feeling. A feeling that something is waiting deep in the forest and watching us."

"That's exactly right," said Everton. "Danger lurking just out of sight."

Jean and Everton strolled to a small side gallery, which contained a selection of works by Sami artists. They stopped opposite a small woodcut of a Sami hunter pointing a rifle at a wolf, which in turn was chasing a reindeer.[3]

"Which is more dangerous, the human with the rifle, or the wolf with his natural weapons?" said Everton.

"I suppose the human is more dangerous because of his bigger brain," said Jean. "If the wolf had a cerebral cortex as large as the human's, he, or she, would be a fearsome predator."

"I agree again," said Everton. "You know, for the entire trip with the dogs, there was probably a creature hiding just out of our eyeshot, following us, watching and waiting. We didn't know it, but he was there. And he followed Vulle and me when we went after Christiaan. Did he go with us to protect Sárá? Was there any benign thought behind the actions of a predator that followed us for tens of kilometres and for several days? Or have I overinterpreted all this, and was it just a wolf out hunting a hunter with a rifle? The memory of it all is sort of fading. It now seems hard to believe."

"Well, our memory for events fades rapidly," said Jean. "The published research suggests that patients and doctors only remember about half of the content of a consultation accurately after several hours. That is why medical records must be written contemporaneously. After weeks or months, our memories become only very approximate copies of the reality we experience."

"You are right about that," said Everton. "The same goes for police records, which are always considered more accurate if written at the time of an incident. What did you think when we came back with Sárá and told you the tale of the giant wolf spirit who saved Sárá with an impossibly powerful and skilful attack? Did you think we were going out of our minds?"

"No. I thought you all believed what you had seen, which is a completely rational starting point. You then interpreted what you saw and spoke about it to each other, and then you reinterpreted it until you found the most rational explanation that you could all share for it all. I wasn't there, so I can't challenge what you saw and experienced. If you were to postulate that a supernatural creature came from the spirit world, followed us around for days, then saved Sárá and killed Christiaan, all because Sárá is a person who can commune with the spirit world, then I might suggest that there could be alternative interpretations of the facts that don't require us to suspend the laws of physics, biology, and chemistry."

"Indeed," said Everton. "But for the purposes of entertainment, the wolf spirit Freki following us around and talking telepathically to Sárá is hard to beat."

The two art lovers laughed together.

The museum attendant sitting in the corner of the room frowned at the two English tourists laughing at her serious picture, which only made them laugh more.

The End

Notes

1 Edvard Munch, *Winter Landscape*, 1898, woodcut on paper, 45.8 x 32.2 cm, Norwegian Museum of Art, Oslo.

2 Edvard Munch, *Winter*, 1899, oil on cardboard. 90 x 60.5 cm, Norwegian Museum of Art, Oslo.

3 John Savio, *Wolf, Sami, Reindeer*, 1922, hand-coloured woodcut on paper. 23.3 x 18.6 cm, Norwegian Museum of Art, Oslo.

Printed in Great Britain
by Amazon